Philly's Bridge

and other Northwest Stories

Whose Woods These Are
Soldier of Fortunes

Written By

Scott Swanson

To request permissions, contact the publisher at:
publisher@villagebooks.com

ISBN: 9798218075750
LCCN:2022919865

Edited by Nancy Tupper
Cover Design by Jill Flores
Cover Photo © Brett Baunton
Layout by Owen Paznokas

Printed in the USA by Village Books.

Village Books
1200 11th St
Bellingham WA
98225

Villagebooks.com

To my *Best of Friends.*
And to my loving wife Betsy,
whose heart lifts me higher than the peaks.

Contents

Philly's Bridge

Scott Swanson

Indian Summer 1981
FINDING THE MOON

Finding the moon through a high-powered telescope isn't easy when you're drunk. Despite my best efforts at drawing a bead, the sly orb shies from the lens, hiding, it would seem, in the much vaster universe revealed by the unblinking eye.

But when I find it, when I catch the cold white edge of the moon, I resolve to compose myself, to hold my breath and set my elbow for the next few tilts and jiggles that will bring the full moon wholly into view, transporting me instantly from this rickety, rolling, midnight porch to the far and distant mountains of another austere wilderness.

Searching the craters of that stark lunar worldscape, I feel like we have just returned from there, Lee and I. I can almost trace our route along the razor ridgelines and shaded valley floors. The contrasts on the mountain were as sharp and vivid, the bright of the sun and the cool, hard edge of shadows. But where the moon is white and silver blue, Shuksan is black and rusty red with pools of aqua green, waterfalls poised in the brilliance of lightning, their rainbowed coronas borne wild on the wind.

From the near vertical perspective of these dizzying heights, I look down upon myself, contorted in this yogi's position, my body hunched, straining with cocked head, craned neck, struggling not to lean too hard on the brittle old spindles of the porch rail. The luminescence of the moon tunnels down through the telescope to print its cratered image on my eyeball, spilling across the polished surface of these thoughts. It shines like a projector's bulb through a thin veneer of memory, revealing time in separate frames like static clips from a movie. As though watching a newsreel, I observe the past happen, detached, disaffected, a student of ancient history.

Eventually though, I'm returned to the present, barefoot, beaten, one iris lit like a cat's-eye marble and pondering, narrating, whispering to myself, "Well, there's one thing Shuksan's got that the moon don't."

And that's Philly, tucked away in a cleft of rock and dripping turquoise ice, more strangely contorted than I am, peering with what kind of eye, through what kind of lens, at what kind of brilliant worlds afloat in space? Lee said he looked like an animal, "like a dead rabbit." It just wasn't Phil anymore.

Just after it happened, Lee and I stood at the top of the ridge, the discordant fluting of cascading water braided like thread on the breeze, twirling aloft on a thermal of wind from the cavernous cleft of the cirque. Far below, the flat green oval of Sulfide Lake caught the gold coin of the sun, and both of us shared the same feeling, the same thought: If souls really do exist, if we truly believe the things we say but are never forced to confront, then Philly was standing right beside us, the ghost of him anyway, T-shirt wrapped around his head like a sunburned, alpine Arab, staring at Shuksan's Pyramid Summit, the vertical walls of the Jagged Ridge and the magnificent 360-degree vista of the North Cascades.

But hell, if that's true, then Philly's on the moon as well. Philly is the moon, as strange and far away. But I don't believe in the moon, at least not the telescope's version. I don't believe our lives are minuscule, dwarfed by a universe of planets and stars so immense we fabricate machines to behold it. Philly is indeed the moon; I can see his features glowing, smiling like the face of Jackie Gleason in *The Honeymooners*. There is the plane of his balding pate, the craters of his wrinkled eyes, the shadowed contours of his bulbous nose and neatly trimmed mustache.

Yeah, it could almost look like Phil, white and frozen like he is right now, up there in that wild and beautiful place where no one ever goes. Except the three of us. And Lee and I—the survivors—departed that ridge with the conviction of never returning, of leaving the cliff, the ice, the high cirque bowl, and the otherworldly aura of the mountain itself as a grand, albeit anonymous monument to the friend who stayed behind.

But *ohhh*, thoughts of moons and universes are too much at this magnification. And this is a magnification, a greater clarity, no matter how much whiskey we use to alter the focus. Lee has returned to the house, drawn to the brighter world of electric lights, kitchen chairs and red-checked tablecloths. It's yellow in there, and warm, with a kind, caring woman who pampers and feeds us and fills us with mind-numbing booze. There are harsher worlds I suppose, but at this moment I just can't think of any.

"How did it come to end like this?" asks the man in the green gym shorts, on the darkened porch, with stars and mountains and moon-silvered meadows across the road. But the grass goes on whispering, the moon keeps glowing, and the cheerful sound of a trickling creek never skips a beat.

Back in the kitchen, returned to the realm of human voices and amber tumblers of twelve-year-old whiskey, I smile and smoke pot and crack jokes like a man obsessed with gaiety. Lee laughs a bit too heartily, too readily, slaps his bare, brush-beaten legs and rambles on about welding, ferro-cement construction, Forest Service bureaucracy. Eventually though, sucked back into the vortex of our misadventure, he offers an image of the body, relates a theory of how it must have happened, and we fade into another pensive silence in the ongoing conversation.

Judy, our unsuspecting host, whom we've never met before and whose only mistake was to be house-sitting at the home of a mutual friend, leads us boldly yet subtly through the dark morning hours, through the barren, lunar mindscape of our grief.

She talks about death, the death she has known, the friends and family she has lost and how all wounds are healed with the passage of time. She opens her heart as though throwing wide a curtain, revealing her life with a drama akin to surmounting a pass, scaling a mountain and discovering a vast, fertile valley beyond. We are strangers to her, crazy people hurtling out of the night to invade her privacy, her much-anticipated solitude. And yet she plunges right in, seeing in us something raw, palpable. She rushes to assuage our pain, revealing her own trials, reopening deep emotional wounds that bleed as profusely as the scores in our flesh. Before we know it, we're pouring out our own stories as well, as if we've known her forever, as though she needed to know our lives in the greatest, most intimate detail.

It's good for us to talk about death, and we say so, Lee and I. Our minds are full of pictures of Philly when he was alive, tossing brush or running a chain saw. I took a picture of him on West Boundary Road, the last image of the man ever recorded, and it was inadvertent. I'd wanted to capture the brush conditions for the report I intended to write, another dry manifesto detailing the performance of our contract. There's a log truck approaching in the background, brush strewn along the road shoulder. Philly is standing at the edge of the photo, tossing an alder or cottonwood sap. He's turned in profile, not looking at the camera, lost in some workaday thought.

Less formal images come to mind, too, snapshots drawn from memory: Philly and I posed naked and dripping after bathing in the rapids of White Creek, combing our hair in the brilliant sunshine, shaking dry like dogs; Phil handing me a demitasse cup of steaming black espresso, or a bubbling glass of Arm & Hammer when his chili enchiladas almost killed me. Or me and Phil on the pitcher's mound, he having walked two guys in a row, me handing him the ball, leaning in confidentially and mumbling, "Blah, blah, blah, scooby doo, and all that kinda shit." Philly walked the next guy too, and Johnny had to yank him.

There's that one rainy day during the planting contract,

Philly trying to roll a joint as Clarke crashed the crummy through a series of potholes. "Jesus fuckin' Christ!" Phil yelled, his wet hands confettied with homegrown. "Slow down, willya! Show some respect for the equipment!" Clarke rocked the truck through another huge puddle and Philly's bald skull hit the ceiling.

"Funny," says Lee, tipping back another shot of Bushmills, "we even talked about dying the night before."

"What did you say?" Judy prompts.

"Scott read us a story from a book I packed up there—something we always do. It was Ray Bradbury, the spooky tale of a migrant family wandering around in the Dust Bowl. They find this old abandoned farm with a dead man in the bedroom. There's a scythe by his side, and he's dressed all in black—he's supposed to be the Grim Reaper. Phil said he wouldn't want to know when he was gonna die, and that if he did, he'd have to start doing something real fast."

"Like what?" Judy asks.

"He never said, and that's what makes it seem so unreal. It felt too fated, too destined somehow when we realized what must have happened, the water jug lying there, his T-shirt on the rocks . . . it seemed too contrived to be true."

"And was it?"

"True? Or contrived?"

"Ordained," she says.

When Lee looks away she turns to me and her blue eyes pose the same question. It's been over twelve hours since Phil plunged to his death, and I still can't accept that he's gone. The Earth has spun halfway round on its axis, in its million-mile orbit of the sun. Wars have been fought, children born, trees tumbled down in the forest. Yet the sound of his voice remains fresh in my mind, his laugh just one bad joke away.

"I don't know," I concede. "I couldn't begin to tell you."

"Try," she smiles, leaning back in her chair, and pours me a shot from the bottle.

We stood in the middle of West Boundary Road. It was hot and dusty, and streaks of sweat striped our faces and sun-browned chests. Two saws lay in pieces and upside down on the tailgate of my blue Ford, the heat from the muffler of Clarke's 41 rippling the sultry air, much like the sun on the hood of the pickup that sat at idle beside us. It was Saturday, September 17, three days before Philly would fall to his death on the shoulders of Mount Shuksan, and our greatest desire at that moment was to finish this final contract of the season, pack up our gear and be off to the high country.

Leaning with my forearms draped above the opened window, I addressed the two occupants of the pea-green Forest Service half ton. "We took a look at your Weedone zone up there. The brush is dead, but it's five feet tall. It's not like you can see through it."

I had to look away to contain my frustration, more acute at that moment than the sting of hot metal on my skin. I was trying to exercise diplomacy, maintaining the kind of restraint I hadn't always managed in the past. The upper half of the road we were brushing had already been sprayed with the herbicide Weedone, which contains 2,4-D, one half of the defoliant Agent Orange used in Vietnam. We'd strolled to the top the previous evening and laughed at the futility of the effort, a waste of time and poison. Ours was a manual endeavor, using chain saws, brush whips, and pure physical exertion.

"Sight clearance," I elaborated, "being able to see around corners so you don't get killed by a log truck. Isn't that what this is all about?"

It was noon, and the neighborhood camp robbers—gray jays— swooped low over our heads, begging for Fritos, chocolate-chip cookies, the usual lunchtime fare. Clarke leaned on the fender of my dusty old Ford, munching gorp from a plastic bag, tossing out peanuts and raisins for the birds that would eat right out of your hand. Even taller than me at six foot four, Clarke was equally skinny, his hair tied back with orange flagging, his wide shoulders burned by the sun. He always ran the oval brush bar on his saw, the kind with the protruding dog that lopped off the stalks like a pincer. He wore a forty-foot log tape clipped to his belt loop, ensuring that our cut-banks conformed to specs, and he owned more boots than Imelda had shoes, weighted with cleats and steel caulks. The cooler half of our negotiating team, Clarke was a stickler for detail, one of my own shortcomings. He collected facts like he did tools or trucks or machines of any kind, his house back in Glacier the tumble-down bunkhouse of a hundred-year-old logging camp. And because he also owned a phone, his home served as the company's office, long distance phone calls logged on the wall, penciled in Clarke's cryptic hand. There, too, we could wash off the job's daily grime in an old claw-foot tub in the yard, a big black umbrella cocked overhead, providing the pretense of shelter.

"Public safety," I intoned, quoting the Forest Service hand- book, "that's what it says on page one."

The driver of the rig was Young Pat, so named because of his youthful exuberance and the fact that he always wore a wide brimmed Smokey Bear hat. His official title was Field Inspector, and the glance he gave his older cohort suggested that my question was beyond his expertise. And who better to solve such a complex riddle than Contracting Officer Dick Smoots.

"Whail," Dick drawled, not so much a country boy as self-conscious city slicker, "that brush shoulda been cut a little lower before sprayin'."

About four and a half feet lower, I could have said, to be in accordance with Forest Service specs. But Dick knew that, and we did too. It was all a charade, an absurd political Monopoly game of forest plans, public appeals, and outright yelling and screaming—which, I'd discovered, didn't help one bit.

The name of our outfit was Shuksan Thinning, a loose woods co-op of Glacier locals currently composed of Clarke, Lee, Johnny, Phil and me. We'd been awarded this job as a result of having been excluded—by "mistake"—from the bidding process that saw the year's biggest roadside maintenance contract go out to mechanical and chemical operators. A series of well-directed letters and phone calls to the Seattle Office resulted in this extra, eight-mile contract, spanning two districts, which we successfully bid at half the estimated "side-mile" price tag. The unusual density of the brush had thwarted our intended profit margin, but we were still making eight or nine bucks an hour in the seventh mile of the contract.

Young Pat was straight out of forestry school, and Smoots unmistakably ex-military. You could tell by his haircut and shiny black shoes, the sharp creases in the legs of his trousers. Lee, by comparison, didn't wear pants at all—or a shirt. Shorts, sneakers, horn-rimmed glasses, and a braid that hung down to his butt: that's what Lee wore, winter, spring, summer, and fall. Rain or shine he rode his bicycle two hundred miles a week, having pedaled his way out west from his home state of New Hampshire. He lived in a ferro-cement "cave" he'd dug in the hillside above Clarke's house, packing up the ninety-pound bags of mortar on his back. The two rooms of Lee's domicile were concave and round, ribbed like stalactites and built around the radiating roots of a monstrous old-growth stump. Some people called him Mister Natural, others called him crazy—but just not ever to his face.

Johnny chose that moment to crank up his saw, and the resultant din necessitated a lull in the conversation. Glancing at the green-clad duo in their aviator sunglasses, he winked, goosed the Stihl's throttle, and returned to work with a song in his heart and foam rubber plugs in his ears.

Not much of a negotiator, Johnny was even less of a vocalist, and the song he was singing—Willie Nelson's "Blue Skies"—was the same one he'd been singing for most of the week, sitting around a campfire, splashing in a creek, or wolfing down platefuls of Phil's rice and veggies. Though Johnny ate incessantly, he never gained weight and was in fact an exceptional athlete, built the way exceptional athletes are built. A well-proportioned Popeye, he rocked from side to side when he walked, his spring-loaded ponytail bouncing while he worked, yellow as ripened corn. He wore a constant smile on his peach-fuzzed face, and Michigan Wolverines suspenders.

I myself was "kind of an asshole," so described by those who'd read my sixty-page appeal of the USFS Environmental Assessment Report—a bogus confirmation of chemical spraying as the most efficient, most cost-effective method of treating roadside vegetation. Hailing from New York—not a place famous for decorum—I guess I'd said a few things, made a few enemies, but I was learning, suffering, persevering. I stayed in their face is what I did, pointing a finger or ratty glove, and that's what I was doing when Johnny had worked far enough away that Smoots could hear what I was saying. "The worst brush conditions I've ever seen," was how I described the job. "A guy might think these roads were chosen specifically to bust our balls. Certainly worse than what went out on the big contract." That's when Phil wandered over, bar tool in one hand, saw file in the other. He wore his sweat-stained, sky-blue T-shirt wound atop his head like a turban, wiry hair the rouge color of rust protruding around his ears. "The worst conditions," he whined, mocking my attempt at civility. "A guy might think . . ." Philly wasn't adept at sarcasm, subtlety never his forte.

"Go away, Phil," I said, "make lunch or something."

"Fuck that," he snorted, elbowing his way in front of the truck's window. "This is bullshit, man," he informed the occupants. "Check out that pathetic spray job up the road. You spent my taxes on that?"

A single stripe of perspiration trembled down Smoots' chubby cheek. It stopped at the first of two fleshy chins and glimmered in a prism of sunshine.

"All you feds got your head up your ass," Phil chided. "And each other's ass at that."

Smoots appraised Phil with a look of disdain, of tolerant, if superior, dismissal. Elbowing Phil away from the window, I amended, "A guy could definitely look at it that way, which makes the fact that we're making a decent wage even more significant."

"Bullshit!" Philly snarled.

"Bullshit yourself!" I snapped back.

Phil was truly beginning to piss me off, a fact of life for our crew. "Listen!" I shouted to all within earshot, "if these roads had been treated on two-year rotations—like they're supposed to be—we'd be making excellent money!"

"Instead of losing our ass!" Phil sneered.

Smoots squirmed a little in his sticky seat, knowing we were right. "Anyway," he continued, avoiding Phil's eye, "you boys are working hard, and I'd just like to thank you for a job well done."

"Hey, thanks!" Phil enthused, struggling to pat himself on the back. "That oughta fatten my bank account!"

What could you do with a guy like Phil? Nothing that was legal, and he wandered away to the tailgate of my truck where he diddled around with my saw.

It was Clarke's turn then, a fresh body, and he questioned Smoots about finalizing the contract, when to sign off, when to receive payment. It fell to me to feed the camp robbers, which I did, tossing the peanuts at Philly as well, who pretended not to notice.

We would finish West Boundary in a couple of hours and be headed to Baker Lake and the final mile of the contract by late afternoon. That made Sunday the final day, also a day when the Forest Service office in Sedro-Woolley would be closed.

"We're going backpacking up the Baker River," I explained to Smoots, elaborating a little on the details. It drained the tension to talk about the trip, conversing with the *bad guys* about something other than the issues, and it made the world seem a friendlier place. It made us all seem human.

"I'll swing by the office toward the end of the week," I said. "Sign the papers before we head home."

Satisfied with the plan, the contracting officer slapped the door of the truck—*Giddy up* being the inference, which Young Pat figured right out. Once they'd left, I wandered over to where Phil was bent by the tailgate.

"What?" he asked, already defensive. "They're laughing at us right now! We're fools to them, out here busting our bony asses for six lousy bucks an hour!"

"We're making better than that," I sighed, not feeling up for a fight.

"Bullshit! You never consider our overhead—equipment costs, maintenance, *depreciation!*"

"C'mon Phil," I sighed, "we're no big-time logging outfit. We're a partnership. We operate on a shoestring—"

"Keep your goddam shoestring! You might wanna hang yourself with it!"

"So quit if you want!" I shouted, failing to keep my cool. "We're not out here to strike it rich, I've told you a million times! We're making a statement! Proving a point! If you don't want to be a part of that then take your goddamn silver trailer—"

"Ah, c'mon," he said, instantly humbled, offering his sheepish grin. "I ain't saying that. I'm not talkin' about quitting."

A breeze funneled up through the corridor of trees, the breath of it cooling our skin, carrying with it the scent of the forest, the fragrance of pitch and duff. A dust devil rose in the middle of the road, conjured from thin, hot air; it danced for a moment in the golden light before collapsing in stifling heat.

"I'm just tired of it, Philly. You knew what you were getting into. You could have skipped this job, but nooo . . . all you do is piss and moan, going on and on about maintenance, depreciation—"

"I know," said Phil. "I know how I am."

I almost believed he might give it a rest, get off my case for a change, when he added, "I just can't see working for less than—"

"Shut the fuck up!" Lee shouted, taking the words from my dry, parched mouth. "Go to work! Let's finish this road and get outta here!"

Johnny started singing in his high, nasal voice. Clarke cranked his new '41. Philly was about to crack the bar nuts on my saw when I grabbed it away from him. "Wait!" he said, "I was just gonna tighten the chain! You can't run it like that!"

"I'll run the fucker with no chain at all and get more work done than you!"

With that I turned and stalked away before Philly could respond, tearing into the thicket of dog hair willow that clogged the tangled ditch line.

We finished a couple of hours later, exuberant and giddy as we headed back to camp. Clarke drove the pickup while the rest of us crouched in the open bed, the wind like menthol on our sweaty skin as the afternoon sunlight fell dappled through trees.

Back at White Creek we changed into shorts and flew at the task of breaking camp, folding the tents, scattering the fire pit, hitching Philly's antique Airstream to the bumper of my blue Ford. The saws and gas jugs remained in the bed, and all the other gear—pots, pans, filthy clothes, MEN WORKING signs and empty beer bottles—were stuffed in the rear of the gold GMC crummy. In less than an hour we were heading back down West Boundary toward Baker Lake and Griner's Cabin Road. Philly and I were in my truck, Phil driving because it was his trailer, the boys in the crummy following close behind because the Airstream lacked legal brake lights.

"Roll 'em up!" Philly enthused, setting the dope tray on my lap, breaking immediately into another Willie Nelson tune. *"On the road again, just a band a' gypsies movin' down the highway!"* he crooned, smiling broadly, adjusting the outside mirror. "It's a beautiful day to be broke and free, the world breezin' by out the window!"

You could never stay mad at Phil for long, that's just the way it was, and I twisted up a joint, stuck it in his mouth, and lit it.

"Now we're loggin'!" he laughed, choking out a cloud of sweet, blue pot smoke. Philly was wearing his straw, silk-banded panama hat and Peter Fonda sunglasses. I'd watched him shave the previous evening, hunkered by the side view mirror, yet twelve hours later his jaw was already stubbled red, nicked by the tracks of his straight-edge razor.

"I thought we were growing beards together," I said, stroking my own week-old bristle. We always grew beards as winter approached, insisting they kept us warm, serving also to make us look tough in the weeks before they filled in.

"Aghh," he groaned, scratching his chin, "the weather's stayed so nice. I hate to give summer an excuse to end."

I couldn't blame him. Philly was right for a change.

Sticking my arm out the open window, I watched my hand soar like a bird on the breeze. That day, like every day the past two weeks, was beautiful and hot, skiffs of white clouds in the clear blue sky like sailboats lost at sea. The leaves were just beginning to turn: orange, gold, fiery red in a languorous Indian summer. It was an idyllic September afternoon as we bumped over the Skagit County roads, headed for a beer stop at the Rockport store before turning west for Concrete and the Baker Lake Highway.

"How long you figure we'll go for?" Phil asked, referring to our intended backpack up the Baker River. More of a bushwhack than a hike, our route would follow the valley floor east to Bald Eagle Creek, then up the flanks of Pioneer Ridge to an elevation of just over 6,600 feet. There we'd enjoy tremendous views of the Picketts and Mounts Challenger, Terror, Triumph, and Despair. It was eight to ten miles cross-country except for two miles of Forest Service trail that ended at the National Park boundary. We'd bring sneakers for wading the numerous creeks we'd have to ford, the route gleaned from Tabor and Crowder's *Routes and Rocks in the Mount Challenger Quadrangle,* as well as Beckey's *Cascade Alpine Guide.*

"Four or five days, I'd guess. Depends on the weather, how much food we eat."

"Why do you wanna go east?" he asked. "Why not head north over Park Butte and into the Middle Fork near home?"

Home, as the crow flies, was just twenty miles away, but close to a hundred on the highway, just the other side of an active volcano. There wasn't much between here and there: timber, clear-cuts, a few farms, the Mount Baker Wilderness. This was a vast, sparsely populated area spanning two counties, bordered by Canada to the north, and Puget Sound to the west. The rest was just boonies with a smoking fumarole at its center, and a rough spine of mountains to the east. Timber production had long been at the heart of things, but that was changing, diminishing as the cities and their populations drew nearer. Yet the dominant feeling was still of the old world: primeval, indelicate, raw.

We'd already had the conversation about where to go backpacking, reviewing my reasons for opting east, Philly's for heading north. It was just another bone of contention in the virtual skeleton of debate that characterized life with Phil, and at that moment I didn't feel like exhuming the corpse.

"You'll see," I assured him. "Pioneer Ridge is gonna be awesome. Lee and I were across from it once on Easy Ridge. Fantastic views into the Picketts, sheer rock spires and creeping fog, like fucking Peru or something. But the view from Pioneer will be even better."

At the beginning of August, Lee and I had attempted to reach Bear Lake, up near the Canadian border, but were forced back by heavy rain at Whatcom Pass. In the midst of our return the sun broke out and we detoured south, forded the Chilliwack River, and camped on Easy Ridge for a couple of days. The view was incredible, inspirational, the crimson sunsets the most breathtaking I'd ever seen, turning the snowfields from pink to red, to dusky, lilac mauve. Easy Ridge also became the perfect vantage point from which to witness the rescue operation of the seven-man Whidbey Island Navy helicopter that crashed into a tower on Mount Challenger, killing all but two aboard. It was a grim, macabre, yet oddly serene experience to sit on the sun-drenched crest of that faraway ridge, enchanted by the physical beauty, yet stunned to witness the aftermath of tragedy, helicopters flashing like tiny bug's wings against the vast, gray massif of Challenger.

Through the binoculars we could see the debris, the bright metal wreckage gleaming in the sun, so sharp against the fire-blackened spire where five had lost their lives. To watch it unfold was like taking a drug, the effect of being drawn into an almost personal melodrama, unseen by others, where death had imposed its stark reality like a black, sooty hoof print on the Earth. Yet it wasn't truly personal. The dead were nameless, faceless people, and we were eating delicious hot corn bread with melted cheese, drinking espresso, and smoking weed. But the sunset ridges fairly gleamed with a tinseled aura, the whole world cast in a mystical, silver clarity by the unsettling proximity of unbelievable, inescapable death. Yet that day's high was nothing compared to the ultra-personal, almost psychedelic quality of the experience awaiting us on the steep, black shoulders of Shuksan.

"I can't wait to get up there," said Philly, pulling into the parking lot of the Rockport store. "I got my rock lens with me. We're sure to run into the Shuksan Metamorphic Suite—Skagit gneiss, quartz diorite, granodiorite. Lots of rock out there!"

"Mountains are funny that way," I grinned, heading for the promise of the air-conditioned store.

The cheerful tinkling of a tiny bell announced our entrance, our eyes struggling to adjust to the sudden, cave-like darkness. A refrigerated coolness radiated from the rolling concrete floor, the pungent odors of suntan lotion and mosquito repellant permeating the low-ceilinged space. Neon beer signs sputtered and ticked, and a rotating cage fan hummed atop a cluttered counter. Fishing lures—spoons and spinners—hung by their hooks from printed cardboard displays, and a Styrofoam cooler filled with ice advertised FRESH NITECRAWLERS, the small white cartons nestled in rows, packaged like Chinese takeout.

Johnny sauntered in behind us, whistling a little Willie, his STIHL cap pushed back off his forehead. He grabbed a twelve pack of Schmidt's with the flying ducks on the label, and a bag of Fritos that I knew were for Lee, Fritos being Lee's only vice in an otherwise puritan diet of cheese, raw vegetables, and beans.

Johnny set the beer on the Formica counter and smacked down a twenty beside it.

"Maybe we should pay with my credit card," said Phil, fingering through his virtual file cabinet of a wallet, "save our cash for emergencies."

Johnny shrugged, grabbed an extra Slim Jim, a couple of Ring Dings and three more bags of chips. Snagging the goodies, and his twenty-dollar bill, he headed back out to the crummy.

"You're welcome!" Phil called after him.

Johnny paused for a second in the tinkling doorway, appraising Phil with a smirk. "What?" he said, "you want a trophy or something?" then let the glass door close behind him.

Phil had recently been awarded a trophy for best defensive player in a county-wide softball tournament. I didn't make the tourney myself, having gone off with Lee to explore Espresso Ridge, but according to Johnny and Tom, Philly had shown some real magic on the mound and justly deserved his magnificent gold hood ornament.

Out of the nine ballplayers in the General Chainsaw lineup, four of us were from Shuksan Thinning: Johnny, the coach; Tom, who wasn't working the road job; Philly; and me. The previous spring had seen us planting trees all day, then driving forty miles to Ferndale to play ball two nights a week. It was frantic but exciting, and we were the only team in the league to take to the field in stagged-off riggin' pants and suspenders.

"Yo, Philly Dog," I said, snatching up a couple of Baby Ruths, "put these on the tab, willya? Don't worry," I added when he gave me a look. "I'll make sure you're reimbursed." But that never happened as things worked out, Philly absolved of all debt.

Back in the parking lot, Phil snagged two beers from Johnny's cooler, and we sipped them as we drove, pressing them to our sweaty cheeks and foreheads, letting the breeze through the opened windows cool our sticky skin. We'd finished them before reaching the Rockport State Park, not a mile away, where we showered in the hottest, hardest water imaginable for just ten cents.

"Damn," said Philly, plopping down at a picnic table, his towel draped over his head. "We'll have to remember this park. Only place left in America you can still get something for a dime."

The sun shone lime on the well-trimmed lawns, glowed fuzzy in the old-growth firs, a pastoral scene with a warm wind blowing, lifting the graceful cedar boughs that partially shaded our table.

"Whaddya wanna bet this whole place is laced with herbicides," I said.

Johnny sighed, refusing to look at me, and snapped the sports section of *The Seattle Times* like wringing a chicken's neck.

"Really," I said, folding my own half of the newspaper, "here's a story about migratory birds in the Midwest being poisoned by a pesticide called Endrin. They're advising hunters about how many ducks they can eat before they're considered *at risk.*"

"It comes from all those corporate wheat farms," Phil added authoritatively, disdaining to glance at the article. "The aerial spray disperses in the atmosphere, gets carried away on the wind."

"Those migratory patterns are ancient," I said, "and how long does it take us to fuck it up, forty, fifty years?"

"Damn!" Johnny grunted. "The Tigers are in last place!"

"Just read some of this shit," I persisted. "The Sea of Galilee is dead. Whole aquifers are poisoned. They find toxic

PCBs on remote Pacific atolls. Pesticides banned in the United States are sold overseas to poor, ignorant, Third World people who can't even read the labels—"

"Enough!" Clarke shouted. "Take the paper away from him!"

Lee did. He'd been lying on the grass doing stretching reps, and he snuck up behind me, snatched the paper, and tossed it in the trashcan chained to the table.

I knew I was obsessed. The job, the appeal, all the phone calls and letters to people who never wrote back were imbedded in my mind like a mental disorder or recurring kind of nightmare. I'd allowed it to get to me. I took it personally, though the whole damn town was involved.

The first time I'd ever even heard of herbicides it was sprayed directly in my face. Johnny and I were working a thinning contract on Kidney Creek, a sixty-six-acre unit off Canyon Creek Road, not five crow miles from Glacier. It was a hot July day, and we were packing our saws and gas jugs up the hill to the road shoulder when a Forest Service spray truck drove by and doused us where we stood by my pickup. We could taste the chemical burn in our mouth, feel its sting in our eyes.

The truck never stopped, just kept on spraying, and after that I began to read about herbicides—the phenoxy acids, glyphosates—and pretty soon the whole town was pissed to learn that poison was being sprayed in the forests around us.

We passed a petition to end the spraying and demonstrated in the highway in front of the District office, letting the Forest Service know they had some real opposition in the tiny town of Glacier.

The whole thing culminated with a bunch of us townsfolk standing in the middle of Dead Horse Road, blocking the spray truck with its deadly cargo of 2,4-D. A week later we ended up voluntarily hand brushing twelve miles of that road, twenty or so men, women, and even kids. It took a few days, but I kept track of our time and expenses, and we kicked the shit out of the Forest Service estimate.

I wasn't there the day of the roadblock. I was with Lee up on Easy Ridge, with the helicopters, sunsets, and death.

At Rockport State Park we drank more beer, rolled another joint, lazed in the brilliant sunshine.

"So who's going," I asked, "to Pioneer Ridge? C'mon, let's see some hands."

Lee had been greasing his body with Wesson oil—cheaper than moisturizer, he says—and his tanned arm gleamed when he raised it. Phil raised his hand too, critically eyeballing the others when they didn't.

"C'mon, Johnny," I coaxed, "you're really not coming?"

"I gotta cut firewood," he said, "make me some money."

And Phil had to sneak in, "Cause we sure ain't makin' it here."

"Don't start," I pleaded, "I can't fucking stand it!"

"*You* can't stand it?" he whined, leaning in my face. "You're the one who don't understand business! You gotta allow thirty percent taxes, fifteen percent maintenance and depreciation—"

"Depreciation," I groaned. "Metamorphic suite! One thirty-second of an inch! Philly, please, give us a break! Give us some fucking peace!"

The one thirty-second of an inch referred to the time when Phil filed the riders of Clarke's brand-new chain after specifically being told not to. "Shee-it," he'd moaned. "I only took it down a thirty-second of an inch. It'll cut way better, you'll see!"

Johnny pulled the towel over Philly's grim face, got up and headed for the crummy. "Better get goin'," he yawned, stretching his back, "before we depreciate."

We gassed up in Concrete before heading north, Philly tipping the attendant kid a buck because he'd washed our windshield and offered to check the oil. Paying by credit card, he slipped the receipt in a neat stack of others on the dashboard, a narrow island of organization amidst the clutter of saw files, bar tools, road maps and candy wrappers. Throwing back his head, the brim of the panama cocked rakishly over one eye, he broke into song again. *"We're the best of friends, insistin' that the world keep turnin' our way! And our way . . . on the road again!"*

We turned north on Baker Lake Highway, passing the Lake Tyee development, and an old homestead where Philly quit singing long enough to describe all the monumental, single-handed feats of logging and mining that some old character he'd read about had accomplished there. We were both into that kind of stuff, pioneering legends, the history of hard work. We swapped logging stories avidly, all of us having worked in the rigging, enthusing about busted mainlines, pulled tail trees, toppled towers. We talked about how the forest industry might change, might actually work and provide jobs, logs, and forests for everyone. We railed about pollution, acid rain, nuclear waste, the chemical madness. Philly said stuff like "depleted ecosystem" and "disrupted biosphere." Somehow, he even snuck in "granodiorite."

"You know," he said, "I don't mean to get on your case about the low bid."

"Really? Then whose voice is it I'm always hearing?"

"Honestly, I realize the important part is making a statement, proving a point. But you gotta actually prove it. You have to make a real assessment, and you just don't know how. You gotta be competitive, understand the costs, the expenses that a real business incurs. You gotta consider the other guy's taxes, his insurance, maintenance and—"

"Depreciation."

"That's right! That's right, man!"

"I understand, Phil, but—"

"No, you don't! You take that out of the nine bucks you say we're making and you ain't got shit! It's like you and Tom going off to cut firewood in your rattle-trap trucks, with no spare tire, or tools of any kind. You never tighten your chain enough! You wouldn't have brakes on this rig if I hadn't adjusted them!"

"Adjust them? Philly, the truck wouldn't move!"

"At least it stops now!"

I had to laugh and nod my head.

"See!" he said. "You know what I'm saying! You agree!"

"Okay," I laughed. "I do agree, in some respects. A guy should maintain his truck, adjust the brakes an' all. But a guy can take that stuff too far. I hardly have any brake drums left! They'll have to be turned for sure. And this shit about running my chain too loose . . . hell, I'd out-cut you any day of the week, and you know why? Cause I'm a much tougher guy!"

"Yeah, right!" Phil laughed, slapping at my leg.

"And because I don't spend half my time fucking around on the tailgate."

"The way you treat equipment—"

"No man, the reason we were pissed when you filed Clarke's riders was because the rest of us had worked a mile up the road, and you hadn't even started your saw!"

"Well . . ." said Philly, sheepish again. "Alright, okay. But what about the other stuff I said?"

"Fine, we'll come up with a formula for figuring a bid that includes all those things, but a little more realistically. We don't need fifteen percent for expenses. More like five, or even two. And we don't own big equipment, Phil—sorry to burst your bubble. And neither will anyone else who's hand-brushing roadsides! Trucks, saws, muscles—they're the only moving parts. And as you stated so well, Philly Dog, this contract is stacked against us. These are not your average brush conditions, and it truly is busting our ass!

"And besides all that, the plain ol' back-breaking, sweat-dripping, hump-busting reality of it is—we can do a better job than those assholes with the poison, and it don't cost the planet a red fuckin' cent!"

"Yeah, yeah," said Philly, reaching through the window to adjust the mirror, tapping it once to make it just right. "I know what you're saying. I told you that."

"Good," I said. "We finally agree on something."

"Yeah, that we're both flat broke," he deadpanned, tugging the brim of his panama.

I sighed, slumped, sat staring out the window.

"That's a joke!" he laughed. "I was only kidding. Lighten up for a change!"

Aqua blue pieces of Lake Shannon glimmered through the old-growth timber, the glacial peaks of distant mountains rising and falling with the road surface, the sun on the windshield expanding and shrinking in starbursts of blinding light. Minutes later we were oohing and aahing, pointing through opened windows, allowing the cool breeze to splash on our faces, envelop our bare, muscled arms. Rounding a corner, the trees leaned away and Baker Lake came into view, the wind off the water invading the cab so that all Phil's receipts blew away.

Arriving at Griner's Cabin Road we jockeyed around until we found a suitable spot to camp, an easy task considering how the flat, sandy expanse of the river now reached nearly to the road shoulder. It also happened to be the trailhead for the two miles of Forest Service trail that marked the beginning of our infamous "hike." We hadn't realized that the final mile of the contract led directly into the next step of our journey, but as fate would have it, the last sap we cut revealed the weathered old sign that read, Upper Baker River Trail, Sulphide Camp, 2 Miles.

Camped along the river about three miles past the lake, we had a nice flat spot for the trailer and a ring of big rocks for a fire. We cut dry wood right off the beach and were headed toward supper in no time. Clarke got the water, Johnny and I carried wood, and Lee ground the espresso beans while Phil labored away in the tiny kitchen of his trailer.

"No damn veggies left," I heard him mumble. "Lee eats onions like fuckin' apples. How does he do that?"

"What?" asked Lee, having heard Phil's remark, as we were always supposed to hear him.

"I said you drones ate everyfuckingthing. The eggs are gone, veggies too. Johnny eats tomato paste straight from the can!"

"Look in the milk crate," Clarke suggested, "with the rain gear, and the roll of chain. I think there's a cabbage in there."

Clarke somehow knew where everything was, maintaining a form of order—distinct from Philly's—derived from his palette of eclectic tastes. Heavy into flatbread and hot Dijon mustard, he could eat a dozen hardboiled eggs at one sitting, hoarded tabouli in Adam's peanut butter pails, noshed on cold baked potatoes for lunch. Once, on a thinning job—it must have been a hundred degrees in the shade—he pulled a hunk of head cheese from his knapsack and offered it around. It may as well have been a head for the reception it received.

"Great," Philly moaned upon finding the cabbage. "Our dinner will taste like Power Punch."

"Perfect for salad," Johnny suggested, "vinegar and bar oil."

The ridges turned pink as the afternoon shadows ascended the hillsides, a handful of planets freckling the evening sky. Down the river about a quarter mile away stood a huge iron bridge. Straddling the main channel and its many small pools and sand bars, it was unconnected to the banks at either end. It stood alone, spanning nothing, providing no access, a pointless amalgam of concrete and steel serving no purpose other than to appear so absurdly and comically abandoned in the middle of the Baker River.

"What the fuck is that?" Philly asked, pointing at the monstrosity.

"It's a bridge," said Johnny. "Get hold of yourself."

"That's the one Young Pat was talking about," Clarke offered. "Remember, at the pre-work conference?"

Clarke and I had attended the meeting as representatives of Shuksan Thinning. We were introduced to Contract Specialist Cam Fellows of Region Six, who was there to deliver a performance manual thicker than *Gone with the Wind,* and apparently much heavier, from the way he perspired. We were required to provide seven shovels, four large fire extinguishers, five small fire extinguishers, four axes or Pulaskis, five hazel hoes, one canteen, and one red-painted toolbox with TOOLS FOR FIRE ONLY printed on its side, with a hasp and padlock so that all the aforementioned tools could be locked away so no one could use them. We had to post EQUAL OPPORTUNITY EMPLOYER signs on each truck, provide the names of everyone on the crew, and submit an estimated schedule of work progress. Cam insisted he'd made the trip up from Seattle as part of the normal course of his job. He always drove two hundred miles to speak with a bunch of backwoods hippies about eight-mile road-brushing contracts.

I didn't remember Young Pat's reference to the bridge, and so Clarke filled us in on the details. A major project undertaken nearly a decade ago, the bridge was intended to provide long sought access to the east side of Baker Lake, a desolate, roadless area where nothing but rugged mountains and old-growth timber stretched all the way to the Pasayten Wilderness.

The bridge had cost some serious bucks, engineered and overseen by the Forest Service. It might even have been some of Cam Fellow's handiwork, one of those five-year, ten-year, or fifteen-minute plans. This one went about six months before the first big flood of the season terminated the contract. The winter's high water wasted the fledgling bridge, stuffing it full of trees, rocks, and root wads until it dammed up and blew out the bulwarks at both ends.

"I like it," said Johnny.

"Avant-garde," said Lee. "Like a huge water feature in a Japanese garden. We should be out there raking the sand. Maybe they'll put out a contract!"

"Stupid cocksuckers," Philly growled, ducking into the trailer with a handful of whole grain spaghetti noodles, returning with a pot of boiling water. "It's just like them assholes. They probably designed the fucker in Arizona, mailed the work orders to Kansas City, shipped the material from Texas, and awarded the contract to an outfit from Florida. Dumb fuckers probably didn't even know it rains here!"

"Shoulda had you build it, Phil," I said, touching a match to the morning's newspaper, setting the kindling ablaze. "Another thirty-second of an inch, the fucker woulda survived the flood."

"I can see you designing it," he fired back. "You'd have it running up and down the river instead of across, nail up a sheet of half-inch plywood and make us drive over it on our way to some low-paying job!" He cracked the spaghetti like ripping a phone book and jammed it into the pot.

Later, we ate cabbage and radish spaghetti with a creamy margarine sauce and kicked back around the fire on the removable rear seats from the crummy. The moon rose full atop the ridge, the ragged silhouette of old-growth timber filigreed in silver. Down river, the steel skeleton of the bridge shone ghostly white, its crosshatch of girders the color of bones. But its derelict aspect felt strangely benign, fitting well within the mosaic of mountains like a blowdown returning to earth, a beaver lodge damming the river.

"I could live in places like this my whole life," I offered to anyone listening.

"It's just this weather," Clarke opined, his disembodied voice rising toward the stars. "It makes everything seem better, grander." He was wearing his square-toed Japanese sandals, his long legs stretched out and crossed atop his Ensolite pad. Lying directly across the fire from me, all I could see were the soles of his sandals, their outline resembling Mickey Mouse ears with the round tops lopped off flat.

"Wait till next week when it's pissin' down rain," said Johnny. "You won't wanna be camped here then."

"Witness our lonely bridge," Lee added, pointing toward the river. "High water must just boil through here. Look at those monster log jams."

"I stay home when it rains," Johnny mumbled, spaghetti noodles bearding his chin. "Burn all that wood I been cuttin'."

"You're like a squirrel," I told him, "a meticulous hoarder of provisions."

"Half a' that wood is mine," Phil asserted, reappearing in the doorway of the little trailer. He and Johnny were sharing rent at the old Harrison place. They always cut firewood together, a wall of it surrounding the ramshackle house like the ramparts of the Alamo.

"Phil's more like a packrat," Lee observed. "A tad neurotic. A lot obsessed."

Phil's trailer was organized to the point of absurdity. *Dainty* was what it was, equipped with all and only those items required for the practical functioning of camp life. But for Phil, practicality took a bizarre turn once crossing the threshold of his aluminum nest, and included within that realm of necessity were cow-shaped salt and pepper shakers, placemats with smiling Dutch girls, yellow curtains with frilly borders, and immaculate, blue-upholstered cushions on the benches aligning the kitchen table.

We, the crew, were forbidden to sit on the blue pillows, as they were clean and firm and devoid of cigarette burns. "My folks might want to visit from Connecticut," Phil scolded, as if the state itself were synonymous with neatness. "I don't want yuz trashin' the place." Thus, whenever the weather forced us to eat inside, Philly would gather the sacred pillows and stash them away on his bunk. "It ain't gonna bust yer narrow asses to sit on a wooden plank!"

But every night when the stars came out and Philly began to snore, we'd sneak into the trailer and steal the blue pillows, stuffing them under our sleeping bags.

"Ahh . . ." Phil sighed, settling on a stump by the fire, a plate of spaghetti balanced on his knee. His balding forehead reflected the flames, the veins there etched in orange. Twirling spaghetti on his pearl-handled fork, he tucked it neatly into his mouth, nodding with personal gratification, daubing his chin with a napkin. He wasn't always into the game, feisty, crabby, looking for a fight.

"Anyway," I said, "I could live in *sunshiny* places like this my whole life."

"Moonlight's not too bad either," Clarke allowed.

"You should have seen it on Espresso Ridge," said Lee. "It was like daylight. You could have read a book by its glow. We actually did, in fact."

It was almost a month ago that day, another full moon and clear as a Chinese bell. We were camped on a ridge over six thousand feet, a mile or two off the trail. Unnamed on the map, the narrow spine overlooked the steep cirque gorge of Mount Shuksan, where Shuksan Creek had its headwaters in the Curtis Glacier. It was perhaps the most panoramic view of the mountain I'd seen, not three crow miles from the Pyramid Summit. The entire route to the top lay exposed: Fisher Chimneys, Winnie's Slide, the Hourglass, Hell's Highway. Glaciers cracked and exploded all day, the sound of them woven with the roaring of waterfalls, the hollow soughing of wind. Dusk turned the summit a lemony chrome, gold as a tooth at its tip, and I offered Lee my recollections of the previous summer's ascent.

There were four of us; two cameras; completely socked in below five thousand feet, exquisitely blue and crystalline above. The sun shone brilliant, difficult to look at, tinted pink through my rose-colored glasses. Shadows ran deep and as dark as tombs in the scalloped maws of crevasses, in the rocky clefts of the narrow Chimney and vertical summit block. It was strangely exhilarating to sit at the top, at once removed from the every-day Earth yet a consummate part of its most primal elements. Otherworldly was the feeling, the ethereal domain of glaciated mountains where humans rarely ventured. Ephemeral, uplifting, it drew friends together in an almost mystical tableau impossible to achieve below, yet simultaneously lonely, contemplative, suggesting the existence, the isolation, of the individual soul.

On Espresso Ridge we drank caffeine and ate cornbread, talking about books and writers, the Earth and politics, the moon, the beauty, and the goats. There were lots of goats up there. With Ra, my dog, a big white Samoyed, we'd snuck up to within a couple hundred feet of a herd of thirty. I shot a whole roll of film, which didn't turn out half as good as I'd hoped.

Departing the ridge next morning, we traversed above the three little ice-filled tarns that had been our stated destination. But the sun burned hot and we yearned to swim, so we labored down over bouldered meadows toward Maiden Lake, a thousand feet below, a clear, glimmering mirror near the green ruff of timber.

The lake was long, oval, perhaps a hundred yards across at its widest point, clear of ice and fantastically swimmable. Cool and refreshing, bracing but not numbing, we paddled naked on a buckskin log out into the middle, floating there in the blazing sunshine, our already-brown shoulders turning pink. Ra followed faithfully along the lake's edge, poetic and forlorn, issuing a staccato of plaintive whimpers that echoed across the calm surface. He was beautiful to watch against the lush green hillside, the wild grasses and baroquely scrolled hellebore, pink and gold monkey flower surrounding the shore adorning his downy white chest. The blue of the sky bobbed in ovals on the water, the sound of our voices carrying, a golden eagle at home on the wind soaring above it all.

"Maiden Lake oughta be . . . straight that way," said Lee, standing before the fire with his arm held out, squinting down its length like a rifle barrel.

"And Shuksan Lake," I added, rising to assume a similar stance, "should be about. . . there."

We must have looked comical posed that way, leaning with our fingers nearly touching.

"Whoa!" Clarke laughed. "Michelangelo!"

"You look like the bridge with your arms like that," said Johnny.

"Yeah," Phil snickered, "washed out."

We laughed at ourselves and sat back down, shoveled more spaghetti in our mouths.

"Good dinner, Philly Dog," I commended.

"Yeah," Johnny agreed, rising from the fire. "Got any more in the pot?"

"Plenty," said Phil. "As a matter of fact, it's all we got left. We're totally outta food."

Johnny staggered, clutching at his throat. "What?" he gasped, propped against the door of the trailer.

"You guys ate everything," Phil accused, quickly relenting, admitting there were enough eggs for breakfast.

"Phew," Johnny exhaled. "You cruel fucking bastard. You gave me a panic attack."

"You should have said something earlier," Lee complained. "Now we have to go back to Concrete, get enough stuff for the hike."

"*Some* of us will be going home tomorrow," Johnny grinned, "snuggling up to the fridge."

"Fuck that shit," I interjected. "We're going exploring! Ain't that right, Philly Dog?"

"Fuckin' A," he replied, revealing his East Coast-ness. "We're headed out where the big rocks grow!"

"Granodiorite, man!"

"Metamorphic!"

"Then we'll be fucking loggin'!"

We were grinning like fiends, teeth lit by the fire, laughing and slapping backs. Down along the river the moon cast shadows through the mangled struts of the bridge. Like negative images superimposed, its shape had lost all definition, as bereft of meaning as it was of purpose, defying recognition. But the night was clear and exquisitely beautiful, as the morning would surely be. Potential storms were not foreseen; clouds went undiscerned. When the moon passed on and the fire burned down and Philly had crept off to bed, all the blue pillows disappeared from his nest, a comfort to us in our dreams.

"Jesus wept!" Philly groaned, swinging a brush whip through the berry cane. "Ain't this what Paul Newman did in *Cool Hand Luke?*"

"That's why he was always trying to escape," said Johnny.

Clarke laughed, holding an actual scythe in his hands, something he'd bought at an auction, or garage sale. "These are the same tools they used in the movie," he pointed out, slicing through the salmonberry with a satisfying whoosh.

"Ya know," I said, about to jerk my 45 to life, "watching Johnny eat breakfast this morning reminded me of the scene where he swallows all them eggs."

"Yeah," said Philly, "except Cool Hand peeled off the shells!"

Johnny smirked and cupped his testicles. "Jewel-Hand Phil," he quipped, "always bustin' another guy's balls."

Cranking the saw, I returned to cutting. We were making excellent time, Lee using a thirty-six-inch bar on his beat-up old 51, leveling the dog hair like dental floss. Our equipment and techniques were unsophisticated, but we moved through the brush with dazzling aplomb, our spirits high at approaching the homestretch. I'd pretty much memorized our hours and expenses, and we calculated the numbers as we worked, yelling over the noise of the saws, primed for the whistle of our collective teapot when the pressure would finally blow off. It looked like we'd make a decent wage—not what we liked to make contracting, but considering what we were up against, we'd come out all right in the end.

Johnny and Clarke were excited to go home, the rest of us pumped about heading into virgin high country. The lines and swirls of the maps I'd been reading floated like pot smoke through my mind, the veins of creeks, the hash-marks of mountains superimposed upon the toppling crosshatch of alder, cottonwood, and berry cane. I existed in that geometric jungle all day, elbows angling into hidden valleys, arms coursed by rivers of sweat, until finally, symbolically, the last sap fell across the trailhead marker and the goal of our contract was achieved. Phil had cut the final alder, revealing the weathered old sign.

In swift, high spirits we tore apart the camp, loading our equipment, hooking up Phil's trailer, leaving only my green tent standing to house our backpacks and gear for the trip upriver.

In my blue pickup with the trailer in tow, Clarke and Johnny left for home. Phil was nervous, actually biting his nails, so worried was he about Clarke piloting his precious silver nest.

"He drives too damn fast. He's got no respect for the rigs!"

Philly had greased the ball hitch, tightened the nut with a box-end wrench, snugged up the shackles in the newly torched holes he'd demanded Clarke cut in the bumper.

"Well, that's the end of the bullshit part," I mused, meaning the completed contract. I felt lightheaded, energetic, unabashedly happy. "Get pumped, Philly! We're headed for God's country!"

But Philly only sighed, rubbed at his neck, paced in a circle as the crashing echoes of Clarke's hasty retreat faded into the timber.

"Forget about it, Phil," said Lee, attempting to cheer him up.

"You forget about it," he snapped. "Let's get to Concrete. Gather supplies. Top Ramen. Beer. Potato chips."

That sounded good to Lee, and great to me.

There's nothing quite like beer and potato chips in the canopied deeps of the boonies. The combination of those two elements, when consumed in actual wilderness, behaves in an alchemical fashion, resulting in an elixir so magical and rare that fairy dust pales in comparison. Besides, stuff just tastes better way the fuck out in the woods.

"Let's hit it," said Lee, the official crummy driver.

A rear-end problem in the gold GMC caused it to grind and thunk loudly when shifted, jolting the entire truck, and Lee was vastly proficient at easing it into gear, driving smoothly over the worst of roads. For this reason, in part, he was relegated the honorific title of Chauffeur.

The other reason he'd landed the job was the result of an incident the previous fall involving an eyewitness account of a "nude man" driving a motor vehicle on public lands. An older woman with grandkids in tow had observed Lee piloting the crummy on our way to a tree planting job, and because Lee wasn't wearing a shirt and also because it was snowing, she'd deduced that he was entirely naked, and proceeded to call the police. Thus it transpired that Lee now drove the crummy whenever and wherever he could, trolling, as it were, for righteous citizens whose morality he might offend. It was lots of fun and made the rest of us feel special, privileged to be chauffeured around these backwoods roads by a potentially naked man.

We headed out in just such a state of anticipation, Lee freshly coated with Wesson oil, myself with a sheen of personal satisfaction. Philly of course was filled with dread, fearful of what might become of his trailer in the hands of the madman with Mickey Mouse feet. And so, considering his state of mind, one could well imagine what went through it when some miles later we came around a bend and discovered my blue pickup, lopsided and leaning at an angle, pulled over by the side of the road.

"I knew it! Goddammit, I knew it!" Phil whined.

Lee pulled over behind the trailer and Philly leaped out before we'd even rolled to a stop. Clarke was standing beside the Ford, one Japanese-sandaled foot propped on its bumper, holding a beer in one hand and a crescent wrench in the other. Johnny lay prone beneath the tongue of the trailer, stretched atop one of the precious blue cushions, smacking the nut of the ball hitch with a hammer.

"What the fuck happened?" Philly roared. "The trailer come loose or something?"

"You figger that out in your head?" said Johnny, pausing a moment in his labor.

"Regular Carl Sagan," Clarke smiled.

"Get offa that damn pillow!" Phil shouted, attempting to yank it loose.

"Here!" said Johnny, easily relenting. "You can get down in the gravel!"

Which is just what Phil did, forsaking the hammer, which Johnny had used to great effect, twisting instead with the crescent wrench, and failing to cinch the nut tighter.

"That's good enough," Johnny advised. "We'll hafta cut the thing off with a torch."

Just then a brand-new, fire-engine red four-by-four diesel pickup squealed to a stop in the road beside us. Its bed was laden with choker cables, acetylene bottles, chain saws and a hundred-gallon pump-handled fuel tank. Leaning from its windows, two old loggers in "timber beast" suspenders and Hickory shirts craned their sunburned necks to appraise us.

"What the hell can we do fer you boys?" asked the driver. Both men clutched cans of Schmidt's beer in their hands, four point-stags on the labels. A brown paper bag shaped suspiciously like a square quart bottle sat wedged between them amidst a clutter of lunch boxes and load ledgers.

"We got 'er dicked!" Phil called from beneath the truck. The bald guy in the passenger seat leaned closer to the window, spit a gob of snoose on the floormat, and eyeballed Phil where he lay on the ground.

"That so?" he deadpanned. "Whose dick are ya usin'?"

The old loggers cracked up, slapping each other's shoulders, hooting, wiping tears from their grizzled cheeks. "Well," said the driver, "if ya need a bigger tool, I'm sure we got one handy!"

Choking on his Schmidt's, his partner sprayed foam across the dashboard, the windshield, and rearview mirror. "You boys want a beer or somethin'?" he managed to ask.

"Hell yeah," we agreed, and the old-timer passed an entire six-pack through the window.

"Anything else we can offer? Oil change? Gear lube?" Glancing at Philly, he added, "K-Y Jelly? Or how about somethin' a little stronger?"

"Nah," said Clarke, "we're driving."

"The hell," said the driver, taken aback. "We was goin' so fast I hardly noticed!" They cracked up again, and so did we, and before we could thank them they peeled off down the road in a billowing pall of black smoke.

"That's Dale Strang!" Philly gasped in awe. "He must be loggin' up here somewhere."

"Think so?" said Johnny. "He might just be practicing."

"Strang's the mayor of Concrete," Phil stated matter-of-factly, ignoring Johnny's sarcasm.

"Really?" I had to ask. "He's like . . . a politician or something?"

"Repub-loggin'," Lee offered.

"The Party That Gets Wood," said Clarke.

"Thinkin' of throwing your hat in the ring?" I asked him.

"Only if it's Phil's panama."

"Har, har!" said Philly, crawling from the beneath the tail hitch. "A real knee slapper! So fuckin' funny I forgot to laugh."

"Amkneesia," said Lee. "Let's hit 'er."

And so we did, the three of us in the crummy following

the trailer in case anything else should happen. But after five minutes on the winding road Clarke was so far ahead he turned a corner and we never saw him again.

More magnificent scenery flew by, mountains, forest, aqua blue water. Phil delivered a sermon on the nearly religious significance of preventive maintenance, repeating the story of the old homesteader for Lee's benefit, and just past the turnoff for the Lake Tyee resort a man was standing by an idling log truck, waving for us to stop. Pulled off in the turnout with its doors wide open sat the bright red four-by-four, the mayor of Concrete straddle-legged in the road, pissing on the Baker Lake Highway

"Take a gander!" said the flagger, the shotgun-riding passenger from the red pickup, who seemed not to care that Lee appeared naked. "Have a looksee!"

Another old logger in a dented hard hat waddled across the asphalt with a log tape clipped to his suspenders. Strang grabbed the dumb end of the tape, and the log-truck driver traversed the length of a narrow stream of urine. "Thirty-nine feet!" he shouted.

"Damn near a peeler!" the mayor cried, zipping up his fly. "That'll go export!"

The highway was striped with similar streams of pee, an assortment of crumpled beer and Coke cans arrayed on the hood of the pickup, along with a half-empty bottle of Kentucky Gentleman.

"Can you fellers top that?" Strang asked, wandering over to lean his hairy forearm on our opened window. "How 'bout it, boys, think you got it in ya?"

"Not yet," said Lee. "Catch us on the way back."

"Yer on!" Strang laughed, moseying back to grab the tape again, the guy in the hard hat trying his hand at it, so to speak. "Thirty-seven!" came the count, "an' that's includin' the snipe!"

"Shee-it!" swore the trucker, kicking a scuffed Romeo on the blacktop. Strang laughed again and slapped the guy's back, towering over his sulking friend.

"I got more deflection," Strang confessed. "Nothin' to be

ashamed of." He raised his beer in a farewell salute as we peeled off down the highway.

"That's why he's mayor," I said, a mile later, "full of piss and vinegar."

The rest of the drive into town we fantasized about global summits in which dignitaries, luminaries, *urinaries* pissed across conference tables to resolve their political differences. "The Salty Talks," Lee dubbed the prospective meetings, as we pulled into the parking lot of the IGA.

A collection of maps was Scotch-taped to the plate-glass windows of the store, and Philly and I lingered there while Lee went inside. There was a Metsker map of Skagit County, an official U.S. Forest Service Mt. Baker-Snoqualmie National Forest map, one of those colorful isometric renderings with mountains and rivers drawn like cartoons, and an honest-to-god three-dimensional pop-out map of plastic lumps and snow-capped bumps with little blue divots for lakes.

Letting myself drift through the thousand printed places, I drowsed in the shadows of Easy Ridge, floated in the oval of Maiden Lake. With the tip of my finger, I read the 3D map like Braille, touching those folded, corrugated places I someday hoped to explore. Had I known then, I could have found the small white bump where Philly would fall to his death, could have felt its protrusion indenting my skin, its meaning relayed to my brain. But I didn't know, and Philly, standing beside me, couldn't have known either. Not on this kind of map, through this kind of window, on such a glorious autumn day.

When we got inside, Lee was literally running up and down the aisles like the FTD man, the only items in his shopping cart a tube of Tom's toothpaste, a package of hair ties, and a red bell pepper. He skidded to a halt when he saw us approach.

"Whoa," I said, "the whole store shakes when you run like that."

The old wooden building was built on the edge of a sandy bluff where the Skagit River might have run at the end of the ice age. Supported by pylons rammed into the earth, braced by aging timbers, it swayed to and fro at the least provocation, like a tree house perched between limbs.

"Let's rock," said Philly, shifting his weight, the meat section rocking with him.

"Gneiss moves, man."

"How suite it is."

"You like polenta?" Lee asked, holding up a five-pound bag of corn meal.

"Afterbirth?" I cringed.

"For the hike. Maybe I'll make some."

"Sounds healthy," Phil sneered, probing through the beer cooler. "Red or white Schmidt's with Italian?"

"Get the cans with the deer this time. Variety's the spice a' life."

We agreed to buy barley, rice, veggies, lemonade mix, and wheat bread. And beer and potato chips of course, the sacramental wafers, the carbonated blood of Christ. We took communion in the crummy long before we reached the deep woods, and by the time we got to the Lake Tyee turnoff and saw the red pickup still parked there, we were laughing hysterically, trying not to wet our pants as we zoomed past the mayor of Concrete at seventy miles an hour. He stood in the highway with one hand on his fly and the other waving farewell.

Munching and gulping our way back to camp, we stopped at Panorama Point, which turned out to be packed with weekend campers. But the beauty of the lake and Mounts Baker and Shuksan bade us to stay and gawk awhile, lazing on the newly mowed grass, strolling barefoot on the floating docks that bobbed with the afternoon's chop. The alpenglow came and did its thing, the mountains responding in kind. Wow, we said, far fucking out, dig that shade of pink. A cool breeze blew across the lake, and for the first time in weeks we felt chilled in our summer shorts. Back in the crummy, I said it again, "I could spend my whole life in places like this."

And Lee repeated, "Only those parts that don't rain."

"Let's stop at the bridge," Phil interjected, refusing to wax philosophical.

It was dusk when we parked and walked the short distance from the road to the pointless bridge. The access spur was overgrown, choked with alder and cottonwood. A narrow deer trail, or teenage beer trail, parted the brush like a tunnel, leading us blindly through the lengthening shadows to a steep embankment at the base of which roared the main channel of the Baker River. It was nearly too dark to see by then, but the moon was rising, poking through the timber, and slowly, eerily, the girders of the bridge began to emerge. There was no way to reach it, a black chasm yawning perhaps thirty feet from bank to steel grid deck. I didn't want to climb on it anyway, to partake of its absurdity. It was reward enough to serve as a witness, to observe from the safety and smugness of distance the extent of the futile endeavor. It was always easy to criticize the efforts of others, especially when their failures were as grand and imposing as a bridge. But in truth, the bridge wasn't built by people like me, or Lee, or even Phil. It was parlayed into being by a sprawling bureaucracy free of personal identity, identical, in fact, to the faceless corporations that saw no one person assume liability, or take responsibility for the deeds undertaken in their name. The bridge existed as a crazy kind of culture sculpture, the non-composting fecal residue of a process that saw no human being, no human necessity take precedence over the theosophy of profit at any cost, with gain the only motive.

Tipsy, light-hearted, potato-chipped out, I said, "I feel like we're actually doing something here, though it all seems a bit like cheating."

"Elaborate, please," said Lee.

"Like maybe it's important that we're doing this contract, trying to prove a point. But it just feels so easy, so unsacrificial—"

"Oh, shit," said Philly, "Saint fuckin' Francis here."

"What are we actually doing," I asked, "bombing around these backwoods roads, sleeping out under the stars? Drinking beer and smoking dope—"

"You actually think we're changing things, like they're sweatin' out in the White House? Whoa, Ron, take fuckin' heed! Lookit what them freaks are doin' up there on Gilligan's Mountain!"

Even in the dark I could sense his smirk, feel his cynical glare.

"Saint Phil," said Lee, "Pontiff of Payroll. Patron Saint of Maintenance."

"Everything's so black and white for you, Phil," I said. "Everything's cause and effect. Drink a beer, it gets you high. Push me, I fall down."

"That a request?" Phil laughed. "Move a little closer to the bank."

"We're talking analogies here," Lee explained. "Try to keep up for a change."

"I get what you're saying, that it's consciousness an' all. How change begins in your mind."

"Something like that," I shrugged.

"You know how I see it?" Philly said, plowing on, not waiting to be asked. "It's just like this bridge here: You make a plan, you build the span, you put 'er in first and cruise across to get to the other side. You don't fly over, you don't dream your way there, and you don't drive around in trucks with no brakes for minimum wage and no food! Cause if you do, you'll end up just like this bridge—totally fucking absurd!"

"Is hope absurd, Philly Dog? How about compassion?"

"Oh, come on—"

"Morality? Ethics? Altruism? All of those irksome, corny words you can't pour in a gas tank, or stuff in your mouth—"

"Hey, we ain't talking about that here."

"Sure we are! That's exactly what we're talking about! That's my reason for being here, what's yours?"

"Fuck man, you make it sound like you discovered the cure for cancer!"

"I've discovered the *desire* to cure cancer, and all the other fucked-up things we do to ourselves and the planet."

"And that's what we're doing, curing all that stuff? And here I just thought we were drunk in the woods."

"We are."

"Well hell then, when does the great crusade begin, or is it already over? Is this a christening, or a ticker-tape parade? A birthday, or a funeral?"

I shook my head, took a swig of beer, watched the moonlight play on the water that rushed and rumbled below us. "You said it yourself, Philly, you start with a plan. You begin with a thought. That's the seed of everything—every job, every bridge, every life."

"Wow," said Philly, "I get it, like what comes first, the chicken or the egg?"

"I know the answer!" Lee chirped excitedly. "To get to the other side!"

"What is the sound of one wing flapping?" I enjoined, trying to lighten the mood.

Lee laughed loudly and clapped his hands, the sound of it carrying out through the timber where some nocturnal creature called back. Lee rarely joined in discussions of consciousness, of the nature of reality itself. His beliefs on the subject were portrayed more than spoken, reflected in the things he did, the foods he ate, the clothes he did or did not wear. We'd discussed it of course, but Lee was reluctant to presume an understanding of the world, to suggest that life was the same for us all.

But it didn't bother me. Rather, I felt elated, lifted above all clouds of doubt to a place where thoughts became crystal clear and all intentions golden.

"It's like the weather," I attempted to explain, employing the recurrent theme. "Moisture rises from the surface of the ocean and gathers into clouds, rolls over the prairies to the peaks of high mountains where it sprinkles down as rain. The drops become water, the water becomes creeks, the creeks become rivers that flow to the sea where it all swirls together again.

"We're the ocean, Philly, you and me, and Lee and Clarke and Johnny. And Smoots, and Fellows, and even Young Pat—except when he wears that dumb hat. It's the collective ocean of our private dreams where thoughts give rise to substance, the puffy white clouds of our purest intent, or whatever we choose to believe in. From that great height falls the whole of our lives as a single drop of rain, dripping from tree limbs to the brim of our hard hats, trickling down our necks. Alone we're the weather, but together we're a storm, or some kind of crap like that. Do I have to prove what storms can do? Do I hafta point that out?" I did anyway, posed on the bank like Sappho's ghost, aiming my arm at the bridge.

Chastened or challenged, Phil lifted his arms with palms upturned toward heaven. "Just pissin' down hope, ain't it," he smirked, "here in the wake of the big brushing contract."

"I can help with the pissing part," Lee offered, unbuttoning the fly of his shorts. "I'm not the mayor, but I'd like to extend a *hand.*"

"Stream of consciousness," I had to add, and even Philly laughed.

We all extended ourselves at that point, relieving mind and bladder, sighing with heartfelt satisfaction as our thoughts were returned to the earth, to the limitless pool of the planetary mind where lives were as yet unimagined.

The following day broke clear and blue. The woods still glistened with morning dew as we wound our way through the trees, arriving at the clearing of Sulphide Camp and the terminus of the Forest Service maintained trail in less than an hour. We'd passed through groves of old-growth cedar and mossy tunnels of maple, their leaves bright yellow, infused with the sun, the vine maple stunningly crimson. Phil had stopped along the way to dispense with the morning's coffee, and Lee and I had gone on ahead, our bladders used to the strain. Thus we were perched on a cottonwood log that had fallen beside the river, discussing our plans or, more precisely, our whereabouts, when Philly finally caught up. The problem was—though we'd yet to realize it—the tree that we straddled had actually landed in Sulphide Creek, and not the river, which was off to the south a few hundred yards, well hidden behind the timber. This was the fabled fork in the road, as well as the course of our lives, the path less taken in what I'll always believe was a deeply personal choice. Not Phil's alone, but ours as well in accompanying him to his end.

"This is the end of the trail alright," I observed, the Tabor and Crowder book opened on my knee. The others bent to stare at the map, though we didn't really need to consult it. We knew the trail ended at a point along the river where Sulphide Creek fed in, and we figured we just hadn't reached it yet, though the path appeared to have vanished.

"Washout maybe," Phil speculated. "We definitely know that happens around here."

"Guess we keep going 'til we hit the creek," I said. "At least we'll know we're on track. So suit up boys, or down, I suppose. It only gets hotter from here."

Intending to boulder our way upriver, Philly and I laced up the sneakers we'd brought for that purpose, his a brand-new pair of Reeboks, me in mismatched Converse All Stars. Tying our boots atop our packs, they increased the weight considerably, Lee's pack already oppressively heavy from the cast iron skillet and lid he always carried when venturing out in the mountains. Lee hated wearing boots, to the extent that he'd designed himself a pair of caulked sandals for logging. He was presently shod in his olive-drab high-tops, mail-ordered from somewhere in Maine, the same place he'd purchased his two pairs of shorts, one green, the other red. Lee's consumer habits were Spartan as Gandhi's, placing one order, once a year, from a single catalog. Last year, to everyone's surprise, he'd splurged and purchased magnets.

Maybe I knew it even then, could sense that we were not looking east but north, that the sheer rock towers that peeked through the timber were not a part of Pioneer Ridge but the south face of Shuksan's Cloud Cap Peak. Or perhaps I didn't really know, though it sure felt funny somehow, nothing foreboding but a bit out of focus, like adjusting the knob of a binocular lens when passed from hand to hand.

But we were all happy as pigs in shit, longhaired freaks in the woods. The water was roaring, resplendent with sunlight like the baubles of a crystal chandelier, the sound of its rushing a chorus of voices that changed with the tilt of one's head. Making our way against the flow, we waded through slow green pools, transparent eddies, hopping from one granite isle to the next while hooting our joy at the timber. Our legs and feet were quickly frozen, our toes too numb to feel, so we stopped on occasion to remove our shoes and sprawl on the sun-warmed rocks.

On one such rock we lay half naked, the massive boulder radiating heat that baked our bodies like bread dough. Above, where the timber began to thin, a smaller stream fed into the creek, too high in relation to the valley floor, prompting me to express my doubts.

"Could that little trickle be Bald Eagle Creek? Why is Mount Blum over there?"

"Lemme see that map," said Lee, snatching the book from my hands.

Funny thing was, the general shape of the terrain above us perfectly matched the contours of Pioneer Ridge on the map. You could have transposed them, one atop the other, and not have noticed a difference.

"Who cares anyway?" Lee opined. "We knew we'd hafta bushwhack, and we're bushwhacking. We didn't expect a trail, and we're not on one."

"I guess," I said. "I was just pumped about Pioneer Ridge, seeing that view of the Picketts."

It was Philly's turn to jump in, to prattle on about how we should have gone elsewhere, north to Park Butte, but he surprised me.

"There's always next year," he tried to console, pointing at the skyline above. "Hell, it's gotta be gorgeous up there."

The ridge to our right was corniced with snow, its rock face serrated black. It grew out of barren talus flanks that funneled into a bowl at the top of the timber. Panning left, to the east, it climaxed in three sharp teeth—Cloud Cap, or Seahpo Peak on the maps, depending on what year they were printed. Running jagged and curved against deep blue sky, the face merged into dustier rouge-colored rock, falling straight for perhaps a thousand feet before tapering into a vast amphitheater where hundreds of veins of cascading water bled into the trough we ascended.

"That's gotta be Pioneer Ridge," I said.

"Maybe," said Lee.

"Let's boogie," Phil grinned, his eyes aglow. "Little bit 'a brush, a jag of scree, then she's all meadow from there. We'll be feasting in the high country tonight!"

Which is exactly what we did, in "Blueberry Camp," but not until after what turned out to be a fuck of a lot more than *a little bit of brush*. Vine maple, elderberry, devil's club, alder, clumps of wiry juniper trees and nearly impenetrable walls of willow. Oddly stunted groves of yew lay crushed by snow to the consistency and effectiveness of barbed wire. It ripped and tore at the flesh of our legs, the muddy sheen of perspiration performing like salt rubbed into our wounds. Some traverses were nearly vertical, the slope so steep and strangled by brush our feet never touched the ground, hordes of black flies so thick and insistent they covered our arms like a sleeve.

Lacerated and scarred by the time we reached open ground, we stopped at a place where a band of smooth, red rock formed a series of ledges like steps, each bench hollowed, indented like a cup, offering spoon-shaped concavities of cold, running water. Some were large enough to float in, and that's what we did, the welts on our bodies throbbing with sensation somewhere between torture and euphoria.

We were exultant nonetheless, each adrift in our own private pool, our personal oasis of languorous relief. "This makes it all worth it," Philly beamed. "A bathtub with a view!"

"I still can't tell where the hell we are," I mused, the map spread out on the rock beside me, anchored by stones in the breeze.

"Honestly," said Lee, "who gives a shit?" his attitude remaining consistent.

"I do."

"Free country," he parried.

"I just like to know where I am."

"You're in way over your head!" Phil laughed and ducked beneath the water.

Phil was in uncharacteristic high spirits, and it was great to see him that way. As much as his moodiness and adversarial attitude could bring you down, drive you crazy, it worked just as well the other way, and one could be buoyed by the sincerity of his smile, the authenticity of his laugh.

Clean and rested, dressed again, Philly with his T-shirt wound atop his head, we headed higher toward the towering peaks and the bright-green promise of meadows.

It was late in the afternoon by then, the sun riding the ridges to the west, a gleaming corona on the sloping ice of what could only have been Mount Shuksan. Near the top of the bowl was a sweeping concavity more of scree than grass, and that was where the game of choosing a campsite began.

"How about here?" Philly kept asking, pointing at any semi-flat spot to pitch my old green tent.

"Up there," I'd nod, my patent response, always wanting to hike a ways farther, a little bit higher on the washboard ribbing of rock. Granodiorite?

"Just another quarter mile," Lee panted, grinning, an inside joke inspired by previous cross-country jaunts wherein my recollection of mountain terrain reduced all distances to no more than a quarter mile, all destinations seeming close at hand, though it took all day to get there.

"Maybe half a mile," I conceded, feeling generous, even a little self-conscious.

It took us the rest of the afternoon and part of early evening before reaching a suitable campsite. We'd traversed some pretty hairy places, following the eroded gullies of cascading creeks, diaphanous mists of freezing cold water billowing over our shoulders, at one point using our fingers and knees to hoist ourselves up a particularly steep pitch.

Arriving at a relatively flat, wide spot, prompted also by the realization that our bodies had no more to give, we threw down our thousand-pound packs and wincingly went about setting up camp. The hour or so before sunset was spent picking berries, gathering dry brush, washing our filthy, bleeding, bodies and cracking stupid jokes. Lee read aloud from the table of contents of Bradbury's collected stories, and I even poured over Crowder's map a couple hundred more times.

By the time the peaks were rouged with dusk we were sprawled out on our sleeping bags, my green tent rippling in the breeze, a fire crackling, and water bubbling. Philly was preparing Top Ramen and veggies, the spicy aroma like nectar on the wind.

"Blueberry Camp," I christened our perch. "A fine place to laze about."

"I wonder how many people have been up here," Lee speculated.

"After that godawful brush hole," Philly groaned, "I'd say not many."

"I bet you're wrong," I said. "I betcha somebody's been on every ridge in these mountains. Someone just as crazy as we are."

"I'll drink to that," said Lee, chugging from a canteen of weak lemonade.

Philly ladled steaming noodles on our plates, spiced with a dash of salt and pepper, garnished with a slice of orange.

"Philly, you dog," I said. "You deserve another trophy."

Nothing tastes as good as hot food in the high country; the same basic principle as beer and potato chips. Or perhaps it was the ritual of friends around a fire that made the feast feel sacred, but whatever the reason, Philly's dinner that night was the best I'd ever eaten, simple and meager as monk's fare.

It was September 19, Monday, and as the crimson washed from the bare rock spires, as a sprinkling of stars flecked the purple eastern sky, no one realized that for one of us it was a final sunset, an eternal night, that the glow on the glaciers and shadows of the ridge bespoke the silent, ceaseless, cyclic passing of a last full moon on Earth.

I read the Ray Bradbury story, sipping hot cocoa that Lee concocted from chunks of real milk chocolate. The moon rose clear of the mountain, casting its ghostly luminescence over the talus slopes, and within the folds of its pearly contrast, the specter of death, in the guise of the short story, crept stealthily into our camp, in the flame-licked circle of orange light cupped like a match in one's hand.

"I wouldn't wanna know when I was gonna die," said Phil.

"Me either," Lee and I agreed.

"You couldn't enjoy anything. It would all seem too serious. Ya know," he added, waxing introspective, "there were places on the way up here where I thought to myself—*if I slip now, I'm a goner for sure.* You gotta admit, it's a motivating concept."

There were times that day when I'd look back at Phil and wonder if he would make it, thinking of all the tricky little handholds, the ledges wide as your toe. But then I figured *nah*, nothing like that ever happens to us, we do this shit all the time. How many days spent out in the riggin', in the side-hill jungles running a saw? And so I'd erased the thought from my mind, preferring to look forward, not back. But I'd entertained the idea of death, existing in my head for whole seconds at a time.

"But if I did know," Phil continued, "I guess I'd have to do something real fast."

"Like what?" asked Lee.

"Wash the blue pillows," I joked.

"I don't know," said Philly, in a non-joking mood. "Just start living a little."

"Party time?" I suggested.

"Shit," he groaned with a lopsided grin. "It's always party time, haven't ya noticed?"

"This is what I'd be doing," I said, "sitting by a fire, turning pale with the moon. I don't believe in the angel with a scythe."

"Who's got the scythe, then?"

"Paul Newman."

Philly laughed, his cheeks and high forehead burned pink

from the sun. But the hollows of his eyes remained pitch black, the shadow below his moustache; it gave the effect of a negative image, a familiar face seen in reverse. As though aware of the drama his countenance inspired, he said, "I really can't tell what's important anymore. I used to, but now . . . I don't know."

Philly was five years older than me, going bald, slightly paunchy, perhaps more than a little weary. From what, I can't say. Life in general I guess, the bullshit we go through each day. "I ain't gonna die, anyway," he assured us, cracking a clownish smile. "No point worrying about it."

"Maybe there is," I said.

"Leave it to Swanson," he waved me off. "Father Sunshine. Enviro-Pope."

"I'm just saying that maybe we oughta be doing something all the time, like we really might die tomorrow."

"Wow, can I quote you on that?" Phil jeered. "So what's this *something* you're doing?"

"I already told you."

"What, sitting up here?"

"Yep."

Phil was skeptical. "What's so special about that?"

"Check it out," I implored with a sweep of my arm, including within the grandiose gesture the mountains, the stars, the rising moon.

"You taking credit for this? Bit of plagiarism, don't ya think? So why even bother with the herbicide shit? Why don't we all just sit here like monks, saving the world from the comfort of our caves?"

"An inside job," Lee snickered.

"The Great Train-of-thought Robbery."

"Really," said Phil, quite serious now. His frizzy hair glowed orange and blue, limned by the fire and lantern of moon. He appeared already half gone from this world, a wandering soul lost in transit. "If we can change everything by remote control, by just thinking about it, then why do we do anything *but* sit around in the mountains?"

"Why didn't I think of that?" said Lee.

"Lee," I felt compelled to remind him, "you already live in a cave."

"You're rambling," said Philly. "You got nothing to say."

"Okay, how's this then? The Earth represents our collective soul manifest in physical terms. With it, through it, we employ the aforementioned consciousness, are employed by it, a part of it, indistinguishable from—"

"The chicken an' the egg again—"

"*To get to the other side,*" I persisted, "of the bridge, Phil, or the road, or the room, whatever we use as the physical focus, the object of our everyday lives. Our thoughts are like hands," I cackled theatrically, flexing my claws in the firelight. "Without them there's no substance to things, no tangible meaning to grasp. But with them we have fingers and articulated arms, tools to give shape to the dream, sculpting the world into mountains and valleys—"

"Mount Play-Doh," said Lee.

"So what do you think?" I asked him, tingling with cosmic imagery. Lee lay on his back in his sleeping bag, lost in its puffy cocoon. He looked like a mummy gazing up at the stars, a pharaoh kicked back in his tomb.

"Hell," he said. "I just don't know."

"So now you're tied with Phil. What would you *like* to think?"

"Well," Lee yawned, rolling on his side, propped on an elbow to face us, "I'd like to think that when I fall asleep tonight the stars will continue to shine, the moon will travel across the sky, and the Earth will spin in a circle . . . that tomorrow we'll walk to the top of this ridge—whatever it's called on the map—and be awed by the absolute beauty of things, not even wondering why."

"Yeah," said Philly, "that's good enough for me."

Alright Philly Dog, I might have said, have it your way. Have this night, this crystalline eve with its hint of eternal rebirth; but just this once, this precious last chance at divining the essence of *something*.

"There's a goat!" said Philly, pointing up the steep pitch above camp. A white dot leaped against a backdrop of gray, and in that brief movement its stout legs, shaggy beard and broad shoulders became discernable.

"Hope he sticks around," I said. "I'd like to get some pictures."

"More white specks on the landscape," sighed Lee, referring to my failed photographic attempts on Espresso Ridge.

"Someday," I said, "when we're rich and famous and hand brushing the I-5 corridor, I'll buy one of those expensive zoom lenses, the kind that require a tripod. I'll even build a garage for its storage, and you, Philly Dog, can maintain it."

"Why not take a picture now?" he asked.

"'Cause Lee's right. It'd just be a small fleck of white."

I should have taken a picture, though. Phil had asked me to a number of times on the way up, but I never did. I wish I'd taken some shots of us that morning, our cheeks and foreheads berry brown, noses peeling pink, me in my green gym shorts and Cascade Construction T-shirt (a picture of Mount Shuksan on the front, GLACIER, WA. in back); Lee in his glasses, long braid and red shorts; Philly like a mullah with his T-shirt on his head and his sleeping bag worn like a robe. Praise Philly! Philly is great!

I wish I had captured the smiles, the jokes, the excitement of the rising sun. But I didn't, and as it turned out, I didn't take a single photo the entire trip, not even at the top. All that remains are those unsnapped images stored in the album of my mind: the spongy moss, the empty water jug, the T-shirt fluttering on the cliff face; Lee climbing out of the frozen crevice where the body lay unseen, washing his hands in the icy runoff, the white snow turning pink.

"Breakfast!" said Lee, serving up a blueberry pancake balanced on his fork. The espresso pot boiled, and Phil set out three little demitasse cups and proceeded to pour. We were truly elegant campers, sopping up syrup, sipping caffeine, our pinkies raised like the white tails of siskins that tittered away on the snowfields. As we ate, we watched the solitary goat climb the sheer ledges with confident ease, oblivious to our presence. This was his home. These were his blueberries.

"Rather superb, all this," I observed, raising my miniature cup. All we needed were monogrammed napkins, crumpets to nibble and dunk.

"Another pancake?" Lee asked.

"No, thank you," I declined.

"Philbert?"

"Certainly," he grinned, holding out his plate.

Eat up, Philly, enjoy this meal, the thick, warm honey and melted butter, a twisted slice of orange. We had it all: good food, good friends, the chill burning off with the sun, a corona of light aflame on the ridges, turning the cirque walls gold. Scattering our meager breakfast fire, we washed our plates with runoff and sand, spitting toothpaste into the ashes. With all our gear securely stowed we headed up again, not to Pioneer Ridge, I knew, though I hardly cared anymore. Whatever magnificent vista awaited would be more than our just reward, would be our comeuppance, our salvation perhaps; would just plain have to do.

The going wasn't rough, and in fact the previous evening's pitch below Blueberry Camp turned out to be the most frustrating leg. Though our route was steep, certain areas requiring some rather passionate rock hugging, there were no real finger hangers, just one foot in front of the other, higher and higher as the view became broader and the sound of the wind grew to whistling proportions the closer we got to the ridge.

We saw more goats far off in the distance, but they always fled before we drew near. The ledges and outcrops were full of their sign: small pellet droppings, tufts of white hair, cozy-looking depressions. This was truly their own special world where we remained curious guests, allowed to partake of its vertical riches as long as we could keep our cool, maintain our balance, existing along the razor edge between rocky spine and air, between the everyday and the infinite. We wouldn't stay long, just enough to allow this strange event to transpire, for a natural act to take place. There was always the feeling of being participants, co-conspirators in some unknowable deed, a mysterious plot that ruffled our thoughts like the breeze through our tangled hair.

But there must have been something knowable about it, else why had I felt so removed, so detached, when finally I reached the top. I got there first, to the narrow ledge that was as far as Philly would go, knowing we'd arrived without looking at a map, at a place that no contour could describe.

"We're on Shuksan!" I called to Lee, who was scrambling up behind me. "Sixty-five, maybe seven thousand feet!"

"What?" Phil panted, arriving at our side.

"We're on the fucking mountain!" I said. "There's the Summit Pyramid! The Crystal Glacier! Sulphide! Shit," I gasped, "this must be the Jagged Ridge! It's awesome from this side!"

Recollections from Shuksan's summit cascaded through my

mind, assisted by all those celluloid images I kept in a basket at home. The Jagged Ridge was a fearsome sight, sheer on this, its southern side, concave walls dropping straight and shadowed toward the unseen cirque of the Nooksack's headwaters. The thunderous sound of a thousand waterfalls spiraled up from its depths, symphonic in scope, magnificent in scale, a crescendo of jubilant nature. I'd read Beckey's accounts of his many ascents of the Ridge, and they'd filled me with awe and a shivering, shameful fear. These were forbidding, inhospitable places, and we viewed them from a perspective that few people enjoyed. It was thrilling, chilling, beyond enthralling, and it was to those sensations that I attributed a feeling of heightened awareness, the conscious experience of life's endless passage that coursed through my body like a current.

"That must be the Nooksack Tower," I proclaimed, pointing a finger at a needle-like monolith of sharp, black rock. "And these three horns are Seapho, what Beckey calls Cloud Cap Peak."

"Guys have climbed those fuckers?" Philly asked.

"Women too, buddy. We're in a helluva place."

"There's the Picketts," said Lee, gazing toward the east.

"Fuck! I guess we're on the wrong ridge!" laughed Phil.

"That one must be Pioneer," I conceded. "Damn, it would have been an ass-kickin' view."

"This ain't too bad either," said Lee, slinging his pack to the ground. "We did good."

Surrounded by glaciers on three steep sides, their crevasses lay exposed, gaping, dirty this time of year, electric blue and aqua green in their bottomless, translucent maws. The roaring of water rose in threads on the wind, plucked like a stringed instrument, the glaciers crumbling, exploding like drums, their percussion delayed by great distance.

We didn't talk much, just listened and watched, our hearts winding down with our breathing. The vista was expansive—Baker, Blum, Bacon and the Picketts, a turbulent sea of sharp teeth. Far to the south was Glacier Peak, and farther still, a vague white smudge in the distance, Mount Rainier. Directly below lay Lakes Baker and Shannon, turquoise planes in the green folds of timber. Out there, hidden in the forests and the jumble of hills, were the narrow, snaking, dusty roads where we'd chosen to spend our lives, ribbons of sweat etched in dirt along our arms, gas boiling over in our saws. But all that seemed tiny from that great height, from such a surreal elevation.

And though it was airy and dazzlingly bright on our rocky promontory, though the reds and greens and silver-blues were stunning in their intensity, something inside me refused to be sated, a sense of arrival denied. I tried to ignore it, thinking of more practical things like where to pitch the tent, where to get water, where to sit and roll the first doob of the day that would dissipate the flutters and seemingly baseless anxiety that challenged Lee's pancakes for mastery of my stomach.

"I'm gonna head up this ridge a ways," I said. "Check out a place to camp." Lee and Phil nodded in wordless consent, and I bounced away like an astronaut released in zero gravity, so buoyant did I feel without my heavy pack.

The ridge narrowed quickly and dropped away, and I had to let myself down a short pitch by the branches of a stunted juniper. To the east of the saddle a small snowfield clung to the sloping ledge. At its nearest rim, runnels of water trickled musically from crusted beards of ice, disappearing into a lush, sodden carpet of bright-green moss. I made my way over and let the snow-tasting runoff dribble onto my tongue. I was parched from the hike up, dehydrated from the copious amounts of sweat that drenched my shorts and T-shirt.

"Water down here!" I shouted to the others, who though unseen, couldn't have been more than a hundred yards away. The thick, luxuriant moss grew on an incline maybe eight feet wide. The pitch steepened toward the edge, dropping away severely over gray exposed rock for perhaps two hundred feet, leveling off into a long, narrow snowfield stained with bright-red algae.

The moss ledge appeared safe, and I moved across it unconcerned, continuing through the saddle and back to the ridge, gaining altitude quickly as I went. The ridge was quite narrow in places, dropping off several hundred feet on one side, a thousand on the other. At one point it widened into a place just level enough to pitch a tent, with enough shallow ledges to create a break from the wind. We would camp there that night, I determined, pausing only as long as the single thought required, continuing up the backbone to see how high I could get before it became completely insane.

The ridge narrowed again, becoming a spine of crumbling, shale-like rock. Suddenly, inexplicably, I found myself indulging in disturbing, terrifying fantasies of falling, seeing myself lose my footing, tipping beyond the point of recovery and—realizing my fate—spreading my arms, tucking my legs and sailing aloft into thin, still air. In slow-motion silence I watched myself plummet, warm wind in the hollow of my ears, long streamers of hair turning honey in the sun as I sank toward the bottom of the bowl.

Kneeling, shaking the thought from my head, I continued on all fours, eventually reaching another drop-off where the ridge fell away into yet another saddle. I probably could have eased myself down, planted a foot, bridged the notch and inched my way back up. Once there, I'd have gained decent footing and could have walked off the shale onto Shuksan's shining glaciers.

But frightened from my imaginary fall, shaken by the degree of awareness the place instilled in me, I sat on a rock and gazed out at the scenery, my scarred knees gathered to my chest, heart pounding audibly in the hollow of my rib cage.

Looking back along my route, I saw Philly making his way down to the first little saddle, a water jug in one hand, the juniper branch in the other. The swatch of blue T-shirt was twisted atop his head like he'd just stepped out of the shower.

Suddenly I was on my feet again and heading back, passing the level campsite, imagining in some corner of my mind where the tent would go, how to maximize the available space, though not quite convinced of the necessity.

Still apprehensive, I moved quickly but cautiously, making sure every hand and foot hold was secure. When I reached the little saddle and skirted around to the mossy ledge, there was Philly with the plastic jug, stuffing it full of slushy snow with a tin Sierra cup.

"Waste of time, Philly," I said. "It'll take all day to melt, and you won't get much water. Taste like shit, too. Be patient. Let it drip into the jug."

"That'll take forever."

"Not quite forever," I smiled, slapping him on the shoulder. "I got a notebook in my pack. I'll rip out a page, make us a little funnel."

But Philly just hmphed and shook his head. Fingering a series of lines in the snow, he irrigated the drips into a larger spout of clear, running water. Smiling broadly, he commended himself, "Now you're loggin', Philly Dog!"

That was the last time I saw him. Those were his final words. I must have said something, made some sarcastic remark, but I really don't remember. There was certainly nothing momentous about it, nothing ominous, or even significant. Taking the Sierra cup, I filled it with slush and headed back up the ridge to where Lee still sat, where he sprinkled a handful of blueberries in the snow and we shared an alpine version of Italian ice.

Sitting there with Lee, I finally relaxed, enjoying our impromptu treat. We bullshitted, laughed, gawked around, generally savoring the moment. We heard nothing, felt nothing, sensed not a thing wrong with the sun-drenched world as we knew it. But there was something happening, maybe not wrong but definitely, irrevocably changed. For at some point in our forgotten conversation, as some bittersweet blueberry squished on our tongue, Philly was falling, tumbling, realizing—maybe frightened, maybe accepting—over the mossy edge, off the ancient rocks, two hundred feet toward the icy moat where I would never see his face again.

After a while Lee and I donned our packs, Lee grabbing Philly's as well, and made to move the relatively short distance to the spot I'd picked for our camp. We eased down the brushy rope of branches, lowering the packs one at a time, and reached the saddle and the little snowfield where Philly by then should have filled the water jug.

But Phil was not there. We scanned the area, searching for some sign of him, some place he might have wandered off to. But there was no such place, there was only the ledge, and the drop off, and as our minds absorbed this obvious fact something alien registered within us. I believe we felt it at the same exact time, for Lee turned to me and we both burst out calling—"Philleeee!" his name echoing across the amphitheater of stone, slow to fade against the vast concavity of granite. "Philleeee!" we hollered again, but no one returned our call.

"Maybe he climbed down to get more water," I said, knowing how futile it sounded. "Maybe he climbed down, and realizing he couldn't get back up, is skirting around the way we came."

That's when we saw the plastic jug lying on its side, half filled with milky water. Inching our way closer to the edge, leery of the sodden moss, Lee said, "Fuck, look at this."

Five distinct lines were scored in the moss, as though from as many fingers, the distinct impression of a grasping hand desperately clawing for purchase. I could only crouch with my head on my arms, folded atop my knees. In the shadows of my body, I tried to accept what must have happened, why it happened, my thoughts returning again and again to the primary question: Why us? Why Phil, and not myself? I thought I knew the answer to the last, believed I understood, for Lee and I both had entertained grave questions about death, or more precisely, survival. In the not-too-distant past both of us had encountered the prospect of death—Lee's in a car wreck in which his companion died, Lee crawling through snow with a broken hip, lying for hours by the roadside; mine in another high mountain fuck-up in which my climbing partner lived, plucked from a crevasse by

Mountain Rescue and another brave helicopter crew.

So it wasn't that difficult to understand why we had been chosen, how off in some gathering front of intent our presence had been requested. Not ordered, or fated, or preordained, but simply agreed upon. Lee and I had consented to accompany our friend to the place and moment of his death; Philly had asked, and we'd accepted, both the least and the most we could do.

"I'll go back around," said Lee. "Maybe you're right, maybe there is another way off of here."

I agreed half-heartedly, peering over the edge, certain there was only one place Phil could be. Standing erect after squatting so long, tiny white dots like mountain goats swam before my eyes, the blood rushing downward, abandoning my brain in a rush of emotional vertigo. "I'll head back up the ridge a ways," I said. "Maybe I can spot something from there."

And so we split up, Lee going down, me going higher. I retraced the steps of my earlier route, turning to look back often, to see whether more of the cliff lay exposed. With a hitch of my breath, I spied Philly's blue T-shirt snagged on an outcrop of rock, silently flapping in the breeze. That was the clincher, it was finally real . . . Philly was gone, his spirit departed, and I just didn't know what to do, where to go, how to cry or scream or do whatever one did at such moments. Was some cosmic vision supposed to appear, a riddle or koan explained, a mystery exposed as all doubt is removed and great knowing revealed in its stead?

Lee appeared then on the rocks below, craning his neck to look up. Skirting the icy rim of the moat he moved slowly, hesitantly, staying close to the cliff wall where the footing was drier, pausing on occasion to duck beneath the cornice of ice. With both arms raised above his head he waved in a gesture of frustration, then cupped his hands to bracket his mouth, shouting words I couldn't quite hear. I waved him in closer, nearer the wall, directing him toward a frozen cleft aligned with the green patch of moss.

Trying to imagine what was going through his mind, I quickly cast out the thought, rejecting the impulse with a shake of my head, dislodging such horrific empathy. His arms rose again in the same perplexed gesture; I waved and headed back down.

On my mindless return along the spine a tremendous explosion resounded from the cornice of the Sulphide Glacier. Leaping toward the precipice, I lay on my stomach to see great chunks of ice tear away from its edge, tumbling in pieces the length of a log truck, the width and girth of a bridge. Striking the steep, smooth walls of the bowl they shattered in a multitude of pieces, the thunder of their impact dispersed by the wind, reaching my ears only after the shards were violently airborne again. They plummeted with a kind of slow-motion drama exaggerated by stupendous scale, one thousand feet down the tapering horn where a green lake lay poised to accept them.

The pristine surface of Sulphide Lake erupted in glittering geysers, swallowing completely the tons of ice that bobbed—just once—before sinking. Rings of gold like bright mountain jewelry was all that recalled their existence, the only remaining observable proof of their centuries spent near the summit. Then there was silence and a scintillant stillness as trailers of ice drifted down, chrome ripples lapping the lake's shoreless edge till they fell back sated, serene.

Lost in that moment with its echo of passage, I at last felt a vague recognition, glad in my heart that for one brief moment I could still be obliged to forget, absorbed by the austere beauty of the planet through which life instilled awe in us all. It was noon of Tuesday, September 20, and Phil had crossed over the bridge.

"He's here!" Lee called, the soft breeze abating, the hot air breathless and docile. Scrambling to my feet I traversed the spine and peered over its other side. I watched Lee vanish beneath a broken rim of ice into shadows as dark as a cave. He returned moments later with his arms at his sides and fingers rigidly splayed.

Kneeling by a rivulet to wash his hands, the snow turned the color of wine.

Only then did he stand and gaze up at the cliff face, his hands now shriveled into fists. "He's dead," he called, and turned quickly away, returning the way he had come.

I was waiting at the first rocky bump on the ridge when Lee climbed up from below. We had nothing to say for quite some time and just sat staring about. We'd known each other for so many years, had made the same jokes and bad puns, that it wasn't surprising when we both said at once, "I just can't fucking believe it."

We laughed for the first time in over an hour, and it made me feel callous and somehow ashamed. But after that it was all we could do, and we laughed at the way the sun fingered the peaks, when a gold eagle soared overhead, when the croaking of ravens carried up from the valley, a hollow sound empty of life.

A few frosty blueberries remained in the Sierra cup, the "Italian ice" long since melted. We doled them out evenly, our purple lips pursed, their taste grown bitter on our tongues. "Thanks, Lee," I said, "for being the one. I just couldn't see him that way."

Just sitting there thinking soon became trying, then exhausting, and finally unbearable. Gray shadows grew to sinister proportions. The hot wind whispered in tongues. We couldn't stay up there another night or even another moment, and so leaving my tent and Phil's backpack behind we raced as if pursued down the mountain, heading toward the fast-moving world of dirt roads that had once seemed of vital importance. I would have left everything, walked naked off that peak, so trivial had possessions become. What required a day and a half coming in took less than eight hours going out. We made our way down in near total silence, stopping only occasionally to rest, eating handfuls of berries in the shade of the timber, gulping mouthfuls of freezing cold water. When our beating hearts calmed and our breath caught up, we'd relate some thought or crude observation that usually devolved into humor. But not always.

"He was upside down," Lee said at one point, "his legs flipped over his head. His hands were broken, and one of his arms. I tried to pull him up but he was just too heavy, wedged between rock and ice. He was absent, dead, like any other animal. It's the only way I could look at him."

I'll always have that picture, its mental image, like the photos I never took. I said, "These are the strangest moments of our lives," and Lee only nodded agreement.

Sun filtered down through the green forest canopy, falling mottled and broken on the trunks of old trees. Everywhere around us were starburst patterns in the branches that swayed in the breeze, a patchwork design of intricate needles and colorful, fluttering leaves. High above us the Sulphide Glacier grumbled its ancient disdain, the afternoon sun gleaming sharp as a sword on the cornice of Cloud Cap Peak. And inches beneath the brown flesh of our chests our hearts beat with furious rage, a rhythm to rival the pulse of the river in its passionate rush toward the sea.

Racing the sun as it retreated from the valley, we splashed like madmen through the same pools and rapids we'd crossed just the day before, still hearing Phil's laughter at his own lousy jokes, swearing at the goddamn flies. We made the descent by remote control, our bodies performing in robotic progression step after mindless step, unaware of how the heat, the pain and exhaustion affected our sluggish brains. In the cooling shadows of the valley floor all intellect was abandoned to a thoughtless will as we found ourselves back on a trail, our minds riding piggyback, dozing like children draped on a parent's strong arm.

Such was our condition when finally we arrived in purplish twilight at the dusty gold crummy parked at the trailhead. Four beers remained from the trip to Concrete, and the familiar *pwisst* of their pull-tab tops marked the beginning of many long hours of drinking, pot smoking, telling jokes and relating horror before sleep would carry us off, easing us down from that narrow ledge from which it seemed we might always dangle, our fingers white and bleeding.

We talked about a million things on the drive to the Sheriff's office in Concrete, weird, metaphysical, all-too-physical things. Why had it happened, why to Phil, and why, oh why with us? We couldn't decide, couldn't agree. But there was a reason; that much we knew. Because without that basic understanding everything else seemed pointless: Phil, the mountains, the herbicides, the Earth . . . nothing was random. All acts had purpose. All life—and death—held meaning.

"I hope so," said Lee, coasting the crummy to a stop at the curb. The window of the tiny Sheriff's office cast a tapering light on the sidewalk. Across the street was the funky old gas station where only days before Philly had tipped the young attendant a dollar. "Here's a buck, kid," he'd grinned. "I like a guy who takes care of equipment."

The Moon Once Found

It's quiet in the kitchen, the rest of the world long since gone to bed. The table is covered with dishes, ashtrays, an empty quart bottle of whiskey. Lee's eyes are closed, though I doubt he's sleeping. You can hear the clock ticking, the little creek gurgling just beyond the window. It feels like the aftermath of a party, or a battle, and the sudden ringing of the telephone resounds with the impact of a rifle shot.

"It's the Sheriff," says Judy, handing me the phone.

"Howdy, Sheriff," I drawl. "You're working late."

He's all business, the Sheriff, and he doesn't seem to give a shit how drunk I sound.

"Can you describe the exact location of the body?" he asks.

"Down to the square inch."

"Are you willing to go back up there, lead a recovery team?"

I can't honestly say that I am—willing. It seems that I have no will of my own, my brain so swollen with thoughts of other worlds, greater realities, that the idea of self has vanished. But the prospect of returning to the mountain brings me back, returns me to my aching body, weary mind and faltering will. "It can't be done," I tell him decisively, and perhaps a bit rudely.

"You'd be surprised what our teams can do."

"You'd be surprised where he's at. The body, I mean." *The body.*

"Why's that?"

"Actually, sir, I was thinking of a helicopter. It's difficult terrain to be carrying things (the body). Lots of miles of bush-whacking. Dense brush. Fast creeks."

"Hmm," hmms the Sheriff. "I don't know that we can get a helo on such short notice."

"How about the Navy?"

"They no longer fly for the dead," he intones. "Not after last time."

"I understand," I tell him, and I truly do, visions of Easy Ridge, the fire-blackened tower of Mount Challenger coming instantly to mind.

"I'll try KVOS-TV," he says. "They fly some recoveries, if they're not too busy. But right now they're tied up with election coverage."

I imagine Dale Strang straddling the Baker Lake Highway, a media chopper hovering overhead. "Check out this donkey!" I can hear him shout, one hand poised on his zipper. "Ya wanna see a real elephant?"

"Are you willing to fly with them?" the Sheriff asks. "Locate the body?"

"Sure, I'll do anything. Whatever I can."

"I'll call in the morning," he informs me. "Stand by the phone."

"I'll lie by it," I tell him, another tired joke.

Lee laughs when I explain about the helicopter and the election coverage. He of course offers the same comic image of the prolific mayor of Concrete.

"Everyone's got a gimmick," I observe.

"Dale's must be huge," says Lee

"Chief of Stiff," our host contributes.

And so it goes, a few laughs, some giggles, but it all fades to silence and the ticking of the clock, and strange, sad thoughts of Philly.

Because suddenly that's all our lives are about and nothing else seems to matter. Drifting back through scenes of the week's odyssey: morning at Blueberry Camp, breakfast with the goats, my fantasy of falling and the avalanche into Sulphide Lake . . . Mexican dinner in the antique trailer, sneaking out the cushions after dark . . . faces lit orange by firefly joints, moonlight painting the bridge.

If there's anything of value to keep from all this it's the thought of Philly's bridge, the idea of purpose, of striving for change, the active intent to do *something*. For if chickens derive from cosmic eggs and hope gives rise to mountains, then Philly really is the moon, and what brilliance it casts is his own. And Philly is the Earth as well, the life and death of which is every bit as intimate and real, acted out in a physical language spoken only in the dialect of souls, those scarred and glorious manifestations of our most personal beliefs.

"Another joint? Shot of booze?" asks Judy.

"Nah," says Lee, "I think today is finally over."

With that we sorely traipse off to our beds, Lee's outside in a Mexican hammock, mine on the overstuffed couch.

"G'night, you guys," says our truly gracious host. "Sleep tight." Flicking off the lamp with the green-tasseled shade, she patters upstairs to her room.

On the first soft surface I've experienced in weeks I swoon at the unaccustomed comfort. All the day's tension drains from my limbs to a throbbing pulse in my head, the lingering taste of fine Irish whiskey making eddying pools of my thoughts. Just outside the opened window the merry little creek is trickling, a star winks brightly in a warped pane of glass, observed through a tear in my eye. The leaves of a maple are dappled silver, suspended like lanterns on the breeze, and falling through branches the moon forms a face, its puzzle parts scattered on the grass.

Whose Woods These Are

Will Quinn's funeral was held at the Grange Hall on the last day of February 1991. A cold front swept down from the Canadian interior and across the eastern plains, shrouding the foothills of the North Cascades with a mantle of frozen snow. It had poured warm rain the previous week, causing havoc in the small mountain towns, and the welcome drop in temperature bridled the rivers and roiling creeks and the muddy brown waters turned milk green.

The hall was an older building with tall, single pane windows and an antique oil stove that failed to damp the cold. Of the fifty or sixty chairs set out, half of them were empty. Quinn was already in the ground, so there was no casket, and no flowers, just a ragtag collection of mostly older men in greasy caps and wool jackets they hadn't bothered to take off. The folding metal chairs looked small and spindly beneath them as they squirmed uncomfortably during the few words spoken by a stout, self-conscious man who was dressed as they were. Quinn had not been a religious man and a church funeral was not deemed in order, nor the words of a pastor appropriate.

Fact was, Will Quinn had not been a likeable man, though to say he'd not been liked would not only be unkind, but untrue. He was of a kind whose life had not gone well, who'd made peace with that fact in that he blamed no other, but who found no peace within himself. There was a time when he'd been happy, and a time when he'd been desolate, but both those times had congealed into a past so obscured by solitude that his wild youth was buried beneath something as hard and shell-like as a scab.

Though not many attended the memorial, and none spoke in fond reminiscence, much was said of him at the taverns where men gathered, and after a number of pitchers had been drunk there were stories told, and if there was not raucous laughter in their wake there were haggard smiles offered, and heads shaken in contrite recognition of their loss.

Will Quinn was a hard worker, a good logger, and at sixty-three he'd been robbed of those rewards deserving of such men who spend their lives toiling in the woods. There were but few pictures of him, and the one that hung on the wall of the Hang Up Tavern, placed there in the aftermath of his death, was taken forty-five years earlier, upon his graduation from high school. In that picture he is young, smiling, and handsome, as is the case in most such photos, especially compared to the weary old men those boys too soon become. Much transpires in the years between, and those who manage to retain those smiles are the hardest workers of all.

In the summer of 1998, with Quinn in the ground most of eight years, a young man in shorts and with a backpack on his shoulder entered the Hang Up Tavern and stood before the wall of photographs that hung there. A hot August day, it was bright outside but cavernous dark in the tavern, and the contrast upon entering took some moments to adjust to.

Standing before the perhaps one hundred frames, he was observed by a woman behind the bar. Ruth Hatch wore a red checked skirt and blouse with cuffs and collar of starched white, her hair dyed a youthful, copper hue that belied the many lines on her face. With a clean rag in hand, she polished a beer schooner well beyond impeccability, studying the stranger with the purple backpack, the back of his neck tanned and sloping into broad shoulders, his ropey musculature well defined against the fabric of a clean white t-shirt.

"You looking for someone in particular?" Ruth asked.

"I am," said the boy, turning to face her, gracing his inquisitor with a smile.

"And who might that be?"

"My grandfather. William Quinn."

Drawing erect, squinting an eye, the waitress ventured, "And who might you be?"

"My name is William Quinn," said the boy, allowing his backpack to fall from his shoulder. "They said I'd find his picture here."

Ruth chose another spotless schooner and began to polish its already sparkling surface. Searching the boy's face for Will Quinn's features, she found them with little effort. The boy's hair was dark and cropped short at his ears, but the shape of his skull could be Will's. His clear brown eyes and blade-like nose were those of a younger man, but there was the echo of Quinn in them too.

"So, you know you're too late by some years," she said.

"I know. I just wanted to see his picture. I wanted to see this town."

Quitting her busy work, sliding her aproned tummy along the bar, Ruth sidled closer to the young man. "How old are you, son?" she asked.

"Twenty-one," said Will.

Assessing the verity of his statement, calculating the years in her head, she thought better of asking for ID and asked instead, "Can I buy you a beer?"

The young man's smile was disarming, and any small-town reticence ingrained in such women as Ruth dissipated at recognizing one of her own. "Coffee sounds good," said Will.

"I'll join you then," she offered.

Seated on stools with the bar between them, Ruth wondered how to ask those questions the whole town might like answered. It was in her to pry, and she was wary of that, not wanting to intimidate the boy, or succumb to ignoble intent. He was not really from here, she reminded herself. There was the city about him, and she didn't want to raise his hackles.

Sipping his coffee, Will glanced out the window as a log truck lumbered by, then another, followed by a yellow crew bus with tanned arms dangling from the opened windows. He said, "My father remembers this town. He remembers the mountains, going there to pick berries with my grandmother."

Ruth went a bit slack jawed, and clicking her dentures, took another quick sip of coffee.

"Your dad remembers Violet?" she asked.

"A little. There are no pictures."

"No," she said, "there mightn't be."

"He says he remembers the dresses she wore, their floral print as she leaned above him. Not much really, just snippets of things, like looking into the sun." The boy laughed softly, revealing again his easy smile. "My dad's a poet," he sought to explain. "He teaches literature at the University. We both live in Eugene."

"Well," said Ruth, "Will's boy did real good for himself. I'm certainly glad to hear that."

Ruth's taxed mind was churning fast, and she wondered exactly what this boy knew, and what else his father remembered. Will Junior—the second Will—couldn't have been four when his mama died. How could he possibly remember the details? Ruth could barely remember herself. "Your daddy grew up in Oregon?" she asked. "After here, I mean?"

"I did, mostly. My father didn't. They moved around a lot."

Ruth just nodded.

"Listen," said Will, "ma'am—"

"Ruth," she implored. "I'm sorry, please call me Ruth."

"I know a little something about what happened. How my grandmother died, and my father was more or less given away. I don't want to put you on the spot. That's not the reason I came here."

"Course not," said Ruth. "I don't think that."

"Actually, I'm just sort of passing through."

Ruth nodded again and, rising impulsively, refilled both their cups. "Gotta look like I'm workin'," she chuckled. "Not like I own the place."

"So, are you going to tell me?" he asked.

Ruth froze with the coffee pot cocked in her hand. "Tell what?" she asked.

"Which one's him? Which is his picture?"

"Oh, Lord!" said Ruth, her voice a nervous titter. "Why, that's him right there!"

Aiming a red painted fingernail at the wall, she pointed out William Quinn's nearly fifty-year-old graduation photo.

The young man stood and followed Ruth's finger to the high, far end of the montage of photos. The wall of glass frames had grown out concentrically from an older, grayer core, pictures of men posed atop logs, or standing on the running boards of trucks, whole logging crews aligned on the wooden spans of complex railroad trestles. Some revealed gaggles of mustachioed men sitting at the bar of the Hang Up, not a one smiling, as was the custom of the day, their eyes all turned toward the camera. Others showed children kneeling on the lawn of a sagging clapboard schoolhouse, captioned between women dressed in wide hats and the billowing skirts of that time.

Will found the photo of his grandfather and saw, too, the likeness of his own father, and of himself. The nose ran strong in the family strain, narrow and knuckled at the bridge, lending Will's dad an intellectual air, conversely appearing raked and hawkish in the already rough countenance of his teenage grandfather. But the eyes were the same, deep and dark, hooded by brows that slanted upward in more of the raptor's likeness.

Will stood for some time before his grandfather's picture, and when finally he turned, Ruth Hatch was watching him and did not glance away.

"He had a place, you know," she told the boy. "Your grandfather owned property out on the Prairie Road." Fidgeting briefly with the worry rag, she added, "They didn't know what to do with it when he died, as no one had heard from your father. You might look into it. Not for the money, but—"

She'd spoken out of place, she scolded herself, had maybe insulted the boy. "I just thought you might be interested," she concluded and, swiping the rag over well-varnished wood, erased the wet rings of their cups. "It's just down the street here, the Prairie Road. Cross them tracks, then over the bridge, some five or six miles out. Name's still on the box. You can't miss it."

Will thanked Ruth Hatch for her coffee and her kindness and stepped outside into blinding sunlight. He stood for a moment on the buckling sidewalk, waiting for his sight to return, then headed up the street toward the tracks and the river and the bridge that would lead him to his grandfather's house.

Midway through the twentieth century, the old forest had been leveled from the shores of Puget Sound well into the foothills of the North Cascades. Pockets of big timber yet remained at the higher elevations, and the mill companies competed ruthlessly for the chance to cut them.

The Second World War had drawn off many of the able-bodied men, and of those that returned some were not fit to log. William Quinn spent the summer months of his youth and the early years of the war wrestling choker cables for gyppos or cutting shake bolts with the Indians. The Sauk and Skagit tribes had largely been banished from the prime river country that had once been theirs, yet were still much sought after and employed for their knowledge of the river and their expertise in driving rafts of cedar to the mills.

Quinn graduated high school at seventeen and lied about his age to enlist in the army. He was on a ship en route to Europe when Germany surrendered, and he never set foot on foreign soil. He remained in the service until his enlistment ended in June of 1947, and returning home took up with a mill company, working in the brush on the new steel towers, and was soon made a riggin' slinger, and then hook tender.

The woods are a fine place for young men with spirit, making the body hard and the mind acute, imbuing the soul with a resolute will as tensile and ringing as a choker bell striking steel. To work in the woods is more than a job, and the forest more than trees. The woods are a way of life that follows one home down the winding dirt roads, through the canopied river bottoms, into town and up the porch steps where it nestles in the wood box, curls from the stove pipe, sprinkling the throw rug with sawdust. So too does it enter the dinner conversations, the small talk at the post office, the grandiose boasting on barstools. All commerce—business and social—is centered around it, from the splitting of shake blocks to the cleaving of fami-lies, the hours, the wages, the everyday gamble with unbridled nature where injury and death take their toll. Still, it is a good life. Young men grow nimble and pliant as alder, then gnarled and mossy as maple, years tumbling from them like yellowed leaves to litter the ground at their feet. Clinging like needles, sinuous as smoke, the woods permeate a town like pitch in the sunlight—malleable, pungent, and rich.

Those early years were good ones for Quinn. He made good money and was respected for his skills, his determination to get wood. He smiled often and was considered handsome by local women, young and old alike, who cooked and shopped and chatted together while husbands and beaus were absent during daylight.

Violet Healy was just such a young woman, and when it became apparent that Will Quinn had taken a shine to her, the wives in town urged her to waste no time in acting demur. There were dances and picnics aplenty back then, and these formed the fabric of polite society. Here Violet was courted by the dashing young Will, walking together in the shade by the river, lounging on blankets furled on the grass, sharing lunch from a white wicker basket.

Cruder forms of social intercourse were found at the taverns, and these were of a male, but not strictly male, persuasion. While beaus and sweethearts danced and courted and fed each other at balls, a wilder, courser, more primal courting transpired at the taverns, or down the road from them, where men with drink and paychecks sought Indian girls whose social fabric was perhaps tanned instead of stitched, made sodden by years of alcohol abuse and venal treatment at the hands of men such as William Quinn.

Quinn was known in both camps, in both gatherings of women wherein skirts were hemmed, or deer hides scraped and fry bread charred over flames. Violet Healy was not aware of Quinn's duplicity, though the older women knew and yet urged the girl to marry. In those dilapidated Indian homes, Louisa Kettle suffered no such communal deceit. She warranted no sudden silences upon entering a room, harbored no illusions of a future with Quinn beyond wild, furtive couplings in pickup trucks, on beer-stained mattresses, or on the bare ground itself.

In May of nineteen hundred and fifty, Violet Mae Healy and William Riley Quinn were wed at a church ceremony that, if nothing else, marked the first and last time Will Quinn would enter a reputed House of the Lord. It was a gay time with many revelers, and Quinn declined to partake of alcohol, though much was offered. He and Violet honeymooned by ferry, touring the San Juan Islands, and were very happy, though much indebted to Quinn's employer for several months to come.

There ensued a period of years in which the couple were much like others of their age and status. They sired a child named William not long after their marriage, and Will Senior was made side rod for his company, cruising timber and engineering logging sites, and he soon bought property on which he built a house for his family. It was out on the Prairie Road, a fine piece of land with a southern exposure and good, potable water.

Quinn loved the woods. He loved being in it, working in it, cutting into it. He loved the smell of it carried on the breeze, ground in the palms of his hands, pitch hardened like quarters on the seat of his pants, fir needles filling his pockets. He loved the look of mist hugging a river, fog drifting up through the timber, sheer rock peaks at the head of a valley ripping great holes in the clouds. He loved to stand on the flat of a stump and imagine the lay of the log roads, the deflection of cables from bull sheave to tail holt gleaming like gold in the sun. The clank of butt hooks was like bells to his ears, the whirring of blocks like birds' song. There was no better life than that which he lived, the respect of his men assured by his confidence, the love of his wife ensured by a son. The very best things were a man's for the taking, and no stronger, steadier hand was poised to take them than William Quinn's.

Violet Quinn was a loving wife and mother who, like all good wives and mothers, placed obedience to her husband and the rearing of her son above all other concerns in life. Her own parents had been elderly, and she their only child, and her memories of childhood were not so much of joy but of watching her parents work. And so, for Violet, work became the antidote to boredom, to anxiety, and an unremitting loneliness.

Her passion was for animals, the animals she'd grown up with, the ducks and chickens and hounds that were her duty to raise and care for, as well as any deer, coyote, or even bear that came out of the woods in proximity to her home. These wild animals her father would shoot at and sometimes, often, kill. A deer or bear could be dressed and eaten, but varmint coyotes were tossed in the truck while the blood still ran from their wounds, discarded some distance from the family farm where vermin could have their way. Returning to the site of these hasty graves, Violet would inter their remains, erecting small shrines made of rocks and sticks and bouquets of roadside flowers.

The birth of puppies was a wonder to the girl, and if one should die she would hide its corpse and bury it with much ceremony, telling her father there were only five pups instead of six, saving its carcass from being discarded or, worse, tossed off to the hogs. And if a hungry coyote killed a chicken, she would grieve for the unfortunate hen but lie to her parents, saying she'd found it lying by the roadside, struck by a passing car. When a black bear entered the yard one morning, Violet stood her ground, waving her arms until it turned away, then pretending the thing never happened.

When Violet married Will she swore an oath of fidelity, and he to her, and their marriage was sanctified by the trust they placed in each other. She loved him as a wife and a woman, dutifully obliging her husband, allowing herself to be taken by him whenever Will was so moved, rocking with him on the springs of their bed, moaning with him when the time came. Their life together those first few years was productive, placid, and plain. Her home was always spotlessly clean, as was the yard and the pens and the profligate vegetable garden, where often she knelt in the long summer months with young Will by her side, shaded by the canopy of whispering corn stalks and towering yellow sunflowers, raking the soil with calloused hands, a handkerchief knotted at her brow.

When neighbors drove by and honked their horns, Violet would glance up from her work, waving in kind, offering a smile until the vehicle vanished in the dust. But when Indians passed, she'd turn away and pull at the weeds with new vigor, avoiding the eyes of the young Kettle girl who might stare from the bed of a pickup. Such an expression could be on the girl's face to remind other women of their grief, women such as Violet, who though down on her knees and with dirt on her cheeks was not quite willing or abject enough to return the mournful gaze.

The young man with the backpack crossed the road and the gleaming railroad tracks, entering a tunnel of cottonwood trees that overhung the bridge. Standing at its center he listened to the water, absorbing the scent on the stirring breeze that moved upriver like a current. Periwinkle, phlox and bleeding heart draped the sloping banks, pools of slow water glowing green in the shallows, in the deep, verdant heart of the summer.

Dropping his pack, Will pulled off his t-shirt to feel the cool air on his skin. His body was tanned from weeks spent in the mountains, he and two friends hopscotching north along the Cascades' spine, climbing pass after pass and peak after peak, camping in a timeless, suspended world of freezing cold lakes, smoldering sunsets and sudden summer rains. The other young men were high on the slopes of Glacier Peak, traversing the volcano along routes gleaned from climbing books and geologic surveys. Will would catch up with them on the high divide that separated the Suiattle River and Agnes Creek drainages, there to continue the journey north.

The mission he was presently embarked upon was more pilgrimage than trek, returning to a place he'd never been but had heard of all his life, a world spoken of so cautiously, even secretly, that in his young boy's mind it had assumed the proportions of myth. While his father had never returned to the place of his birth, Will could not keep away, and so when his college friends and climbing companions suggested the trip, he had eagerly agreed, the rugged heart of the North Cascades only half the mystical, fog enshrouded universe he wished to enter.

Passing beyond the shaded bridge, fields of lupine and bell-shaped foxglove furled like quilts in the checkered sunshine, rolling foothills rising behind them, the final buttress before the peaks. The hills were thick and deep with forest, here and there scarred to rich brown soil and ringed with fire-blackened timber. Solitary clouds appeared tethered in the sky, more balloon than kite in the stillness of an August afternoon.

Will passed fine old houses, ramshackle trailers, gray barns bent as if shouldering a wind. Bulldozers, log trucks, and dinosauric logging towers sprouted like weeds from the yards. Through the rippling heat that rose from the asphalt he read the hand-painted names on the mailboxes, some of the lettering flaked away, so long had the same families lived on the land. Crickets hopped desultorily along the graveled road shoulders, shattered beer bottles winking green and brown in the dried-up mud of the ditch.

When a car slowed down and stopped beside him, two teenage girls giggled their way through the invitation of a ride. The car was a beautiful white convertible, as fine a renovation of a classic Pontiac as Will had ever seen. He wondered how such young girls could be driving it, but accepted the ride with gratitude, and with his pack at his side, his arm looped around it like a prom date, he luxuriated in the wind-blown comfort of the rear while the pretty girls laughed and squealed, plying him with questions. Their bare arms lay tanned and draped on white leather, their sun-bleached hair like coronas on the breeze. The thump and hiss of whitewall tires rivaled the music from the radio, the wink of sun on polished chrome like stars come out at noon.

The Ptarmigan Traverse, Will told the girls when asked what he was doing in the mountains. Will Quinn's old place, he casually replied when asked where he was bound. But Mister Quinn died, they were loath to inform him, smitten with sudden angst. "I know," said Will, which restored their spirits, and they resumed their joyful, adolescent bouncing to the staccato beat of the road surface.

"What's it like in the city?" the blonde passenger asked, sliding her sunglasses down her nose, revealing startling blue eyes.

"It's all right," said Will. "What's it like living here?"

"Definitely not all right!" the driver giggled, and both girls erupted in laughter, their arms snaking out to slap at each other in what Will imagined was a friendship forged of youth and isolation. "I can't wait to get out of here!" she added, her pink tank top failing to hide what appeared to be a hicky on the golden slope of her shoulder. "I'm moving to Seattle. Someplace with lots of people!"

"You must go to college," the other remarked. "Whatcha taking?" she asked, not waiting for confirmation.

Will explained that he'd begun as an English major, then switched to Geology, but was currently considering Philosophy. "You don't look like a philosopher," the blue-eyed girl said, allowing herself a glance at Will's bared torso. Both girls collapsed in another fit of giggling, and Will had to laugh along with them.

"Well, I plan to grow a beard," he joked.

"Oh no, don't!" the two of them pleaded, and dropped him off in a pawl of dust in front of the old Quinn place.

Ruth Hatch had been wrong about the mailbox. It lay in tall grass on the stump of its post, the victim perhaps of an errant snowplow. But the name Quinn was still legible in black painted letters on its side, and though the rusted flag was sticking up and the jaw-hinged door lay open, Will found only an old bird's nest within. Seeing his name on the mailbox somehow thrilled the boy, and through the mirage-like distortion of sun-baked asphalt the Prairie Road seemed to ripple away into an imagined past as storied as that of Lewis and Clark, disappearing into a time when everything and everywhere was wild, unspoiled, untouched, vibrant with natural beauty.

The sloping fields of the valley floor shone gold in the summer's heat, writhing like waves in a furtive breeze, and the boy shouldered his pack and headed toward the house. The driveway had seen traffic of late, tire tracks etched in the chalky dust, along with the transient hieroglyphs of tiny, taloned birds' feet. Will spied an old fence line hidden in the weeds, its gray posts corrugated with age, starred with frilly lichen. Starched yellow grass lay bent and ghostlike, defining the wire strands, like jerky left to dry in the sun, desiccated over time.

The house, what was left of it, sat less than a hundred yards from the road. Its windows, once boarded, were long since broken and sheets of weathered plywood lay delaminating on the ground. Its facade was a patchwork of shingles and clapboard and tatters of tar paper gone pewter in the sun. The roof was much the same, woven of shakes and rolled asphalt, with buckled sheets of galvanized metal near the hole where the chimney had been. Stepping between the ribs of what had once been a porch, Will peered through the frame of a window. The floor inside was warped and rolling, strewn with glass from the shattered panes and beer bottles tossed by teenagers. A crumbling pile of brick and mortar marked where the hearth had been, spot lit by the gaping hole in the roof where sunlight angled through. An open fire had been lit there once and the floor joists showed black and scaly, bristling with rusted nails.

Dropping his pack, he straddled the sill, tested the strength of the floorboards with his boot before leaning through and standing in a place where his grandfather, grandmother, and father had all once stood. Disturbed by his entry, coruscating motes of slumbering dust rose golden in the shaft of light, lending the room a spectral, otherworldly quality. The silhouettes of absent picture frames were traced on faded wallpaper, ovals and rectangles of old-fashioned roses revealing where once they'd hung. There was a decaying smell, and a urine smell, and in the rotting rafters where the sun shone through the cone-shaped nests of yellow-tailed swallows clung to the sagging roof, mounds of their feces on the wasted floor tufted with downy feathers. A table and one chair remained in the room, positioned by a window where a rag of curtain blew. The window looked out across the fields where the receding shoulders of timbered mountains scalloped the far side of the valley.

Will looked through that portal as if into the distance of his grandfather's past, imagining the many hours the man had spent gazing through it at the ancient landscape, so familiar to him they remained in his vision even after his eyes were closed. How must it feel to have such roots, he wondered, to be of such a time and in such a place that the sameness of things lent credence to the idea that, as fleeting and insignificant as a man's life may seem, it was somehow connected to something greater, a tiny piece of the flowering quilt that billowed out and over those ridges toward the larger life of the planet.

Such was the feeling that Will sought, even at the tender age of twenty one, and he'd hoped that by returning to the secret core of his family's past he could gain some insight, make some sense of his own feelings of attachment to nature and to mountains that drove him ever further into them, and onto them, in a thirst for wildness that often went unquenched at the summits of towering peaks.

Wilderness, he believed, was the landscape of the soul, his own and that of the planet, and in its absolute perfection could be sensed the transient nature of reality itself, the vitality of it, the health and goodness manifest of its obvious, beneficent self. If only he could convince himself of his part in it. If only every mountain he'd climbed had been a mile farther, a yard taller, an arm's length closer to that handful of sky in which he could literally feel the dance of atoms, to grasp as if with groping fingers his personal role in the vaster reality that played out so magnificently around him.

Looking around at the disintegrating house, he could not imagine his father living here. That William Quinn was a fragile man, a bookish intellectual whose sense of beauty derived from journals and paintings, whose experience of nature was taken from the haiku of Basho, the prints of Hokusai, whose wilderness flowed from the pens of Gary Snyder and Barry Lopez, and whose outrage at the desecration of Nature's beauty led him to donate his time and his money to myriad environmental causes but who never once ventured into wilderness itself, keeping it always a separate thing, excluding himself from its primal reality in a way so obvious, even to a young boy, as to make his son feel great sorrow for his father, for the denial he showed of his heritage.

Will himself could not get enough of the woods, the rivers, the lifeblood of the mountains, though from his father he'd also learned a love of books and art and ideas. The walls of his childhood bedroom were lined with volumes of Whitman, Frost, Thoreau, and Sandburg. The journals of Aldo Leopold and the travels of John Muir were his Hardy Boys, the photographs of Edward Curtis and Darius Kinsey displacing posters of Ken Griffey and Kurt Cobain.

It was said that familial traits often skip a generation, and he wondered whether that might not be true of his family, what little he knew of it. And what little anyone knew was here, he told himself, standing in the derelict house, trying to take some feeling from it, struggling with the decrepitude of the place, the desecration it suffered at the hands of time and drunken high school kids.

Hearing a vehicle pull up outside, he leaned by the window to see a tall, shiny four-wheel drive pickup idling in a cloud of dust. The truck's sole occupant was an older man in a peaked cap, with a ruddy face and squinting eyes that swept the front of the house as if searching for something, or someone. For me, Will sensed, and stepping back through the portal of the same broken window, he approached his apparent inquisitor.

The truck was red and meticulously clean, polished to such a glossy sheen that Will could see himself in its door panel, his bare legs and torso elongated, his head cut off by the opened window and replaced by the round, silver-haired face of the driver. The truck's bed was lined with chrome diamond plating where a bright orange chainsaw lay snuggled in a crate, nestled as if to hatch an egg amidst a bunting of chaps, cork boots and rubber raingear.

Will was anxious. This was not his property, and thus he was a trespasser. Yet there was something about the logger's gaze that held curiosity instead of rebuke, amity instead of malice, and so Will nodded and said hello, and the old logger, a man in his seventies with bright eyes and a morning's worth of white whiskers, touched the brim of his cap in return.

Turning off the engine, the man in suspenders and long-sleeved shirt swung down from the cab, his booted foot catching the rung of the sideboard with confident, practiced ease. He wasn't a tall man, but stout, barrel-chested, and when after a moment of silent appraisal he extended his hand, his grip was like to crush the bones of an unwitting, unwary acquaintance.

"Randall Toffness," said the man, by way of introduction. "Randy's fine."

"Will Quinn," said the boy, and the two men nodded at each other.

"I know who ya are," said Toffness. "I just spoke to Ruth. Whole town knows by now."

"That's okay," Will grinned.

"Nothin' to be done about it," said Randy.

"That's all right," the boy repeated. A long moment passed in which neither man spoke, then Will said, "So, did you know my grandfather?"

"Sure I did. We all knew him."

"You were friends, then?" said Will.

Randall Toffness pursed his lips. "No man was Quinn's friend. But I was his neighbor."

By the look on the boy's face Toffness saw he'd hurt him somehow, or at least confused him. "It was Quinn's own choice," he explained. "He chose his solitude, and he kept it. We were not ill disposed toward one another, and we helped each other if need be, but that was all."

Observing the boy digest what he'd heard, Randy decided he needed clarification, a fairer picture of his grandfather.

"Quinn was an honest man and a hard worker," he said. "He held no grudges and kept his word, and he didn't belittle or speak ill of others. He just didn't speak to them. Understand?"

Leaning toward the boy, he held his gaze as though his meaning showed in his eyes, and as if the young man found it there, he slowly nodded his head.

Both men chose to look at the ground, studying the toes of their boots. Ravens squawked and croaked overhead in surveying the timbered hillside, the whoosh of their wings distinctly audible as they rolled and tumbled through the air. "Hot day," Toffness offered, pinching the brim of his cap, lifting it off his balding forehead to swipe at the sweat with his wrist.

"You working in this weather?" the boy asked, reminded of the chainsaw.

Toffness broke into a wide grin. His teeth were tiny but the real thing, his cheeks blushed pink by broken capillaries and sunburn. "Oh hell," he said, "I'm as retired as they come. Here, let's have us a beer."

Reaching through opened window of the truck, he withdrew two cans from an Igloo cooler with the digits of his club-like hand. Using that arm to point toward the shade of the disintegrating porch, he said, "Hell, the kids are always drinkin' here, might as well join 'em."

Will propped his pack against the wall where it lay and leaned against it, the older man lowering himself with some delicacy onto the splintered wood. "Gawd," he swore, "when you get to be my age, every little move's like a three o'clock gettup." Will smiled, and the first tug of ice-cold beer solicited a welcoming sigh. Randall Toffness did likewise, and for a moment they sat in comfortable silence, letting the shade and the afternoon breeze dry the dampness from their brow.

"You live nearby?" Will asked.

"I own where you're sittin', boy. Make yourself at home."

Looking at the man from the corner of his eye, Will remembered what Ruth Hatch had said about the property. "I have no interest in this land," he informed his new acquaintance, in case such a thought had occurred.

"Make no difference if you did," said Toffness. "I own it free and clear." Then, thinking better of it, he added, "Of course, a man my age, if you were in mind to buy it back . . ."

Will shook his head. "No," he grinned, "I'm just passing through. Actually, I'm here on a climb." Laughing, the boy raised his beer in the air. "I know it doesn't look like it now, but that's the reason I came. Or it's supposed to be," he added. "But I don't really know anymore. I don't know why I'm here."

There was silence again for half a beer, then Toffness brought the conversation back to Will's climbing. Will told of the summits he'd climbed with his friends, and what peaks lay ahead.

Toffness listened with rapt attention. He said, "I used to firewatch when I was a kid. Way back in there, up on them ridges between east and west. They used to run sheep up there, you know, and there were still a few grizzlies left to eat 'em. There was mining claims, too, and crazy old codgers who'd shoot if you got too close. That's what they said, anyways, though none ever shot at me.

"You'd have liked it back then," the old-timer sighed. "I bet you'd have liked that life."

Will could sense he was being appraised, compared to his father's father.

"Too bad you never met him," Toffness said. "Too bad he never met you. It mighta done him some good."

"Dad told me a little," Will allowed, not to keep the man guessing.

"How he was more or less given away, there being no family around."

The old man shook his head. "Not a proud chapter," he muttered.

Will didn't speak. If Randall Toffness had something to offer then that would be his choice, but he would not ask him for it.

"There were plenty of folks would have taken the boy. We're not a heartless people. We keep plenty of truck with our own." He was looking at Will as if to find solace, some acceptance of that fact, and it shocked Will a little to realize it. For a moment the beer felt too cold in his throat, though by then it had gone lukewarm. Looking away toward the foothills again, into their distance and the removal it suggested, he wondered if he hadn't made a mistake in coming to his grandfather's house. Maybe there was something here he didn't want to know. Maybe the age-old mystique of his heritage held not charm, but chagrin.

Randall's big hand slapped hard on his arm and Will jumped as if jolted awake. When he looked at the old man there was none of Ruth Hatch's comic reticence in his eyes, and Toffness said, "Well, do you wanna know, or not?"

In the winter of 1954, Quinn's side was logging a patch of old growth far up the Suiattle River drainage. They had a fine landing on a high knob above the river and were strung out a good thousand feet across the draw, with four extensions on the inch and seven-eighths mainline. They were bullet logging, and the roads swung around nicely, tail holts plentiful and stout on the far side, and deflection sufficient to suspend a heavy turn. In fact, the yarding came so good that the riggin' crew soon caught up with the bushlers, a predicament that brought a joyful pride to the slinger and his chokermen but promised to halt production if Quinn could not hurry the cutting along.

The bushlers were a savvy bunch of tarheels who knew their business and got good scale from what they felled. The holdup was a single fir, fully ten feet at the butt and leaning toward the river at a precipitous angle. They'd beveled the thick bark down to bare wood and the wedge cut revealed it to be punky at the heart. In the days of the railroad loggers such a tree would be left or leveled with dynamite to clear the way, but times had changed, and some still remembered the indigence of the Depression, and the sound portion of such a great tree brought good money.

Smaller trees had been felled in the lay of the giant, grazed past it purposefully to knock snow from its crown. The snow also promised a softer landing, saving it out for greater scale and bonus cases of beer.

Quinn arrived as the back cut went in and wedges driven behind it. The saws were McCullochs with six-foot bars, and two men were required to pack one through the brush. They cut and wedged, cut and wedged, and still the fir would not lift past center. The bull buck finally called for jacks, and they notched and jacked to no avail as the spongy wood absorbed their efforts. Quinn helped, swinging a maul, never one to stand idle, and when a jack piston reached the end of its throw, he drove wedges to free it, then shimmed it in place to begin anew. The river behind them thundered through the gorge, the huff and groan of the yarder above echoing within it, and the bushlers were obliged to shout above the din as they knelt in their tin pants in the snow. Quinn could hear the whistles coursing through the timber, their meaning conveyed by their number and order, and when the hook tender loped through the brush to assess the bushler's progress, Quinn swung his maul harder, faster, the excitement of the work equivalent to sport, the responsibility like gravity.

In the midst of such activity, in the middle of a jack change, a wedge of green wood bubbled and popped and the weight of the two-hundred-foot tree sat back on Quinn's hand. It pinched off three fingers—knuckles, palm and heel—so cleanly that when Quinn held it before him, in the words of one bushler, it resembled a fresh bite of pie.

Were it not for the quick wits of the bull buck and the hook, Quinn would have bled to death, but they tied off his arm with his sleeve and a twister and tight-lined him to the landing in a stirrup of mangled chokers. Quinn was unconscious for the ride down the hill, and it was just as well. They flew down the icy, mud-rutted roads in the primer-gray '48 Dodge, and inside of two hours had him in a hospital, where Quinn was to spend the next three weeks delirious with fever and pain. They saved his hand, what was left of it, and when he returned it was as shiny and black as a small pistol, with only his thumb and forefinger remaining. Quinn pointed it as such, as much to his own temple as at those around him.

Through the remainder of that winter Quinn was in much pain, both physical and mental, which he tried to assuage with pills and alcohol and staying out to all hours with his cronies. If the physical pain abated the other only increased, as Quinn understood he would never again work as he once had, that the scabrous talon he called a hand would never withstand the weight of a saw, or a tail block, or suffice even to pull steel strands through a cunt splice.

As summer came on and the logging picked up, there were fewer men left to drink with, and some say it was then that Quinn took up with Lou Kettle again, if ever he'd left off. The Indians had summer camps along the Suiattle, where they lived in quick shanties and dried salmon on vine maple racks. Fires burned throughout the night, and though the tribes reveled in their ancestry their lot was also one of poverty, and alcohol, so Quinn fit easily in their midst, and if it seemed he mostly lived amongst them the fact would prove difficult to refute, as he rarely appeared at his home on the Prairie Road.

The white women in town spoke of him in their way, and if Violet Quinn entered a store or cafe with young William in tow they regaled her with good cheer, without questioning her plight or inquiring about the health of her husband, which was just as well, as Mrs. Quinn, much to her dismay and secret anguish, knew little of him.

Violet worked in her garden through the hot summer months and the fruits it bore would have been legendary had not later events eclipsed them. Young William grew willowy and berry brown as he scampered amongst the flowering pea poles and trailing nasturtium vines, floppy-eared puppies nipping at his heels from the litter whelped that spring.

Will and his mom often walked together to the new bridge that spanned the Sauk, standing at its center to watch the green water rolling beneath them. There was always a breeze there, and maybe, by chance, they might see Will's father drive by, the bridge forming that bottle neck of divergent cultures through which all things eventually passed. Only once did Violet observe her husband, and though his pickup slowed it never stopped, and she saw on his face such a look of shame that she felt less sorrow for her abandoned son and more for his tortured father, crippled as he was in both body and soul.

It was never in Violet to hate anyone or any living thing, and any such feelings akin to blame were reserved solely for herself, not so much for her actions, which were always forthright, but for her eventual belief in her own delusions, fabricated as they were to ensure the survival of all those creatures around her.

Though nothing like the farm she'd grown up on, the house on Prairie Road was an efficiently run, self-sustaining enterprise, due largely to Violet's unceasing labor. In the year after Quinn's accident, the company checks arrived monthly and faithfully from his employer, but this was the only help she received outside of her own great efforts. The garden was bountiful beyond any standard, and the livestock—chickens, a few ducks, goats, and a milk cow—were healthy, prodigious, and well sheltered. In this endeavor, the care of the animals, that aspect of Violet's nature that might be labeled eccentric was most observable. The chicken coop, rabbit hutch, and milk shed were fortified to an extent that seemed contrived not only to protect the domestic stock but their predators as well. The chicken coop was skirted by scraps of sheet metal buried and back-filled some two feet in depth. Three strands of wire formed an enclosure around it, and flags of bright cloth were knotted to the fencing, as well as tin cans filled with pebbles or nails that rattled at the slightest provocation. Scarecrows garbed in outrageous fashion—often more stylish than Violet herself—populated the lot like a fairground. Only the most courageous or desperate coyote would attempt to dine at the Quinn place, and the dogs would set off such a bellowing reception as to warn the whole valley of their presence.

Quinn himself ceased to be admired by the community and instead became much reviled, ignored by fellow loggers who'd once worked with him, and for him, adjacent barstools at the Hang Up Tavern often vacated as soon as Quinn sat down. He fought a great deal, his claw of a hand not diminishing his fury and the ability to make it manifest. He survived on nothing and for nothing, and like all creatures without purpose he learned to loathe himself and what he saw of himself in others. Other drinkers were his first targets, and of these there were many. Quinn's face was often as purple and swollen as his hand, the claw suffering greatly in the process, the ER doctors who stitched his wounds warning that he'd lose the hand if he continued to use it as a weapon. Quinn never listened, if even he heard, and went right out and fought again, sleeping it off at the Indian camps where the Kettle girl, in her solemn way, felt somehow obliged to accept him.

The next winter put the previous one to shame. The snows came early and lingered late, accumulating to depths that none of the loggers could plow through or grade away in getting their trucks to the landings. Many were shut down, and with it their incomes, and the taverns were loud and prosperous with the chits that men signed, of which most were known to be good for. The Indians survived as they always had, in ways that white men were loath to imitate. Their junky old trucks with clanking chains were seen nosing through town, laden with purloined shake blocks. The shake mills were always the last to close, and at dusk of a gray, snow mantled eve the great steel teepees burned red against white, yellow smoke shrouding the silent hills as ash drifted low over rooftops.

In the depths of winter, it was not unusual for extended Indian families to live together in one house, the stove always burning, a venison stew simmering on the warped steel plates. Some of the elders still danced, and at sites along the river, in the lee of ancient cedars where the snow was loath to drift, they built towering bonfires and gathered about them to sing.

Quinn was one of those singers, though mostly he mumbled along with the tune, if tunes they could be called. With his good hand wrapped around the neck of a bottle and Louisa Kettle tucked beneath an arm, he was as happy there as he was at the tavern, if happiness was ever his lot. The pain never left his half a hand; it traveled up his arm through the knotted tendons of his shoulders, eventually finding its way to his heart where it fed the even greater pain that always burned there, the pain he felt for his miserable life, for the shame he'd brought to his good wife and innocent young son.

Pain was an element continuous in the abstract, like rain or snow or sunshine, coming as if from someplace above, soaking, freezing, or searing the flesh that had little to do but absorb it. When he looked at his hand, at the evil, crescent shape of it, he was overwhelmed by the desire to plunge it into his withered chest like the talon that others named it, tearing from himself that organ of pain that pumped anger, despair, hostility to the far reaches of his body where it curled in a fist and crashed down on weaker men around him, infecting them with its cruelty, drawing their own pain like blood from a wound and pouring down, down, down, like rain, like tears, like snow.

The snow was piled deep around Violet's house except where she'd shoveled it away: a path to the woodshed, to the coops and hutches, wherever her daily chores took her. The County men who plowed the roads had cleared her driveway, and for that she'd given them corn bread, fresh from her oven. Her husband had not been lax in cutting years' worth of firewood, and the house was warm and safe. Young William played by the crackling stove, the pups now grown and scattered about him in comical attitudes of repose, sprawled on their backs with their legs splayed wide, floppy hound's ears scarfing their snouts as they snuffled and twitched in a netherworld of dreams.

The animals had been fed and watered and Violet sat knitting at the table by the window. Now and then she glanced up from her work, enchanted by the view from her small domain, the few sheds, the snowy fields, the timbered hillside and cozy valley that appeared on occasion when the falling snow parted like a shawl. But always it chose to close again when the spiraling flakes resumed.

During one of those dreamy glances Violet spotted movement at the edge of the woods, in the bowered darkness of the timber where the fields began. Seeing it again, she reached for the old army binoculars that hung from a nail by the window, hoping to catch a good look at a coyote, or perhaps, by some miracle, a wolf. But the creature that emerged from the shadows was neither. It was a bear, tall, rangy, anxious and dark against the virgin whiteness. Forsaking the binoculars, she reached for the rifle that leaned by the window. As the cold of its barrel leaked into her hand she watched the bear's approach, its shaggy head swinging from side to side, its progress advancing in similar fashion, a meandering switchback of blue in its wake.

When Violet heard the milk cow bellow, she rose with sudden resolve.

"I'm going out back a minute," she told young William. "Stay here, stay warm. Keep the dogs with you." Throwing on a ragged wool Mac of her husband's, she stepped out the door with the weapon.

The rifle was a Winchester 30.30 and Violet knew how to use it, though she'd hoped never for such a purpose. Chambering a round, she moved along the shoveled path toward the milk shed where the bear had been heading. Reaching the red painted corner of the building she leaned to peer around it. The bear, she saw, had come to a halt and was looking directly at her, perhaps thirty feet away, its great head swinging from side to side. Standing to height on two hind legs, its frame was considerable, though thin to emaciation. What had awakened it from winter's sleep, or if it had wintered at all, Violet hadn't time to consider as the creature gave out with a savage bawling that echoed off the doors of the barn. Turning to look where the bear was focused, Violet saw the pups, four of them, all of nine months old, pouring from the opened door of the house where her son stood clad in pajamas, the doorknob in one hand, a piece of corn bread in the other.

The dogs charged directly at the bear and a terrible caterwaul of growls and yelps and baying erupted that was like to loose the snow from the surrounding forest. The bear spun round in defensive circles as the pups charged and feinted and charged again, until their blood stained the snow in great cursive loops and their torn bodies flew willy-nilly, landing in steaming, entrailed heaps on the pock-marked plain of white.

When the bear turned to Violet, bawling deep in its throat, she at last raised the rifle to her shoulder, so terrified and dumbfounded had she been rendered to witness the slaughter of the pups. Yet still she could not pull the trigger, and as the bear snapped and whoofed and the cow bellowed in its stall, a sudden blur of umber streaked across the snow, and the speckled bitch, who had stayed with William until that moment, threw herself at the bear, which batted her away with a single, ruinous swat.

Violet backed toward the barn with the rifle poised, and the outraged bear moved with her, falling forward the length of its body then rising again on hind legs. Once more she retreated, and the bear repeated its truncated charge, and when she moved again the bear had halved the distance between them. That's when Violet heard her son speak, and glancing sideways saw him standing in the icy pathway, one bare foot atop the other as he repeated his singular plea—"Mama?"

The bear roared with the bark of the 30.30 and the first shot had no effect. Ratcheting the action, Violet fired again, then again until the bear appeared to stagger, then again and again until it tumbled in the snow, firing until the great creature ceased to move and steam failed to issue from its snout.

Gulping a long draught of Kentucky Gentleman, Quinn threw the empty bottle in the fire where he should have heard it break, but where it only melted, so hot were the coals, the well banked temperature of a forge.

The elders had long since gone off to dream, but the young men and their women drank on, seemingly oblivious to the cold. The moon was hidden in layers of the storm that raged and abated at will, its luminescence enough to delineate the revelers and the hoarfrost fringe of the river. The snowfall would slow and then stop altogether and the valley walls appear, steep and pale, shrouded with reverence until the snowflakes swirled again.

Louisa Kettle was a quiet woman, her silence a hard lesson in alcoholism and its propensity to infect whole families, whole tribes. The final smallpox, the addiction had been called, the slow gift of incremental death. But Louisa was loved, if not by Quinn then by the members of her family, loving each other in their fall from Nature's grace. Though who's to say what Quinn really felt, whether in his way he loved the girl in the same way he loved his wife: from afar, from a distance more than miles and more like the breadth of sensation, a retreating horizon like the curve of the Earth at which he could never arrive.

Or maybe Quinn never loved at all, had never been touched by the feeling. But Quinn could be touched, that much he knew. He knew it by the way he felt in the woods, how moved he was by its beauty, the grace of a river as it coursed through the hills, the sound of southering geese, a tiny shrew unearthed by a turn, cowering by the toe of his steel-caulked boot. There was something like that in Lou Kettle's eyes, in the fact that she rarely spoke, or smiled, and his ability to reveal his true nature to her was only half because she was Indian. Her love for him, though unreturned, was what allowed him to be wretched around her, which Quinn was never courageous enough to display in the presence of his wife.

Violet's beauty was of a kind that could not be seen at first glance. Her smile was fetching, her laugh winning, but those were superficial things and had not the depth of beauty he found in the quiet things she did—her gardening, her knitting, her care of the stock, her forgiving way with their son.

But Louisa Kettle was forgiveness incarnate, pulling the

stitches from Quinn's scarred brow, dragging him out of the river, saving him from his venal, volatile nature and soberer men at the bar. Louisa was also beautiful in her way, though not in the flatness of her features. Like Violet she was strengthened from the life she had led, surviving year after hard won year, man after selfish man.

But when Quinn was drunk Louisa's forgiveness seemed more like tolerance, like pity, a weakness he found abhorrent. Or if not forgiveness, it was acquiescence, so complete in its surrender it comprised defeat. How pathetic was a woman who allowed life to happen to her, who allowed life to be done to her, a whore of random circumstance. Her beauty at those moments was not her own but that of her people, made tragic, and therefore magnificent, by their despair.

On and on he went in his mind, caught between those ever changing, self-betraying notions of beauty and vileness, his own, that of women, that of nature, that of the bottle through which all things shone with a mellow, amber glow. When Quinn staggered up from the snowy bank where he'd gone to vomit, where he'd gone to think his venomous thoughts, and saw the small round face of Louisa Kettle beneath a man whose quivering buttocks shone in the firelight, he kicked the man full in the kidneys, rolled him aside and pulled Louisa from the frozen ground by a hank of her hair and after that beat her senseless, and all who tried to stop him were themselves beaten, so frenzied was Quinn's madness, so thorough his resolve.

Quinn awoke in his home on the Prairie Road where he hadn't been for most of a year. The fire had gone out and he could see his breath, and he couldn't remember how he'd gotten there or why he'd come. His fists—all one and a half of them—were bloody and sore, so he knew that he'd been fighting, but that in itself was not exceptional. What was exceptional was his presence here, in the house he had built himself, and the absence of his wife and son who did not answer when finally he called their names.

A pan of corn bread sat on the stove and the sight of it, as did most forms of nourishment, turned Quinn's stomach. There were drops of blood in the hall and he followed them to the kitchen where first he saw the Winchester leaning against the range, and then the speckled bitch, wrapped in bloody bandages and laid out on a rag-tied throw rug. The dog was alive, but just barely, and Quinn resolved to shoot her once he'd learned what was afoot.

Taking the rifle from where it leaned, he cleared its breach and sniffed its bore: it had recently been fired and left uncleaned. Quinn was too hung over to feel panic, but some facsimile of concern swept through him and he made a quick perusal of the house. Nothing.

It had quit snowing and, glancing out the window, he saw something by the milk shed that made his blood run, and with the rifle in hand he went out to inspect. The dogs, the bear, the tracks in the snow told him much, but not where his wife and son had gone. Peeking in the barn the Guernsey was there, and the goats stood staring from their pen. Everything appeared in its natural order, or near as he could remember.

When the sheriff arrived some ten minutes later, he heard a rifle shot and trudged around the house to find Quinn standing over the body of the speckled bitch, the rifle extended in one hand. He arrested Will Quinn for the near murder of Louisa Kettle, then listened to Quinn's story of what he'd found at the house and what he believed to have happened, right up to where his family had disappeared.

The sheriff, an acquaintance of Quinn's on different counts, became anxious then, and handcuffed Quinn and put him in the rear of the squad car before calling for assistance. There was a strangeness about the scene that unsettled him: the gory tableau of gutted animals, the numerous, oddly dressed scarecrows shrouded in snow. When help arrived, they performed a thorough search of the property and found the young boy bundled in wool blankets and hidden in the craziest-looking chicken coop they'd ever seen, its open walls fluttering with colored rags and rattling tin cans, surrounded by multiple layers of chicken wire.

A week later they found the body of Violet Quinn near a bend of the Sauk River about a mile below the steel bridge from which she'd plummeted. They ruled it a suicide, though some were never convinced, and William Quinn, though cleared of assault charges—the Indian woman refusing to cooperate— would always remain, in the eyes of many, guilty of killing his wife.

The carnage at the house on Prairie Road, Quinn's savage beating of the Kettle girl, and the sheer strangeness of discovering the young boy in the chicken coop combined to make the

State's decision to wrest custody of William Quinn Junior from his father an easy one, and to further decide, in the absence of kin, to remove the boy from his father's influence entirely by placing him in a foster home in another county. Quinn, completely dispirited and consumed with guilt, made no attempt to dispute the decision, and hence the malicious and long-lived contention that he'd given away his own son.

In the years following the death of his wife, Quinn sunk further into morbidity, drinking as he'd done before but with an even greater passion for self destruction, stealing shake blocks to afford his whiskey, withdrawing entirely from the circle of his peers in which he'd once held rank. He lived with Lou Kettle in her dark home, which he further darkened by hanging blankets over the windows, resorting to the half-light of kerosene lamps. He spent many hours in their meager glow, with bottle in hand and horror in mind, imagining the last hours of his wife's sad life: witnessing the slaughter of the hapless pups, emptying her rifle into the bear, dragging the wounded bitch to the house and administering to its obviously mortal wounds. And then, for reasons Quinn was certain he'd never fathom, placing their son in the chicken coop in some . . . what, hysterical, demented, even mystical attempt to protect him? From whom, he wondered. From him?

When he thought of her journey to the bridge that night, as it must have been dark by then, trudging through the snow, pulling her collar close about her, slipping across the icy, nearly transparent grid of the span, the black water roaring beneath her . . . he remembered the day he'd passed them on the bridge, Violet and William, Violet's gaze following him as he drove slowly by, turning on her heel to keep him longest in her sight. She'd been waiting for him, he knew, as she had on many other occasions when Quinn spied them first and pulled over into the trees, waiting for them to leave, or turning around after several minutes and retreating the way he'd come.

Had she waited for him that final night? Had that been the

purpose of her otherwise senseless journey, as if sense could be taken from such an act? Had Quinn just missed his wife's demise? How long after her leap had he driven by: an hour, half hour? One minute? And if he'd beaten Louisa only half as savagely as he had, could he maybe have saved Violet's life?

In the spring of 1961 Louisa Kettle died in childbirth. The child died as well, much deformed, much maltreated in its gestation, and its death was considered a blessing. Quinn was not so deluded to believe the child was his. Louisa had lain with many men, and Quinn felt no anger or betrayal in that. He was a rare lover to her anyway, so debilitated was he by drink and slothfulness and depression. There was little left of Quinn by then, nothing worthy of preserving, yet even with the grim hand life had dealt him, both literal and figurative, some small part remained that was made even more desolate by her loss.

He had no money, and no place to go, and so in an act of shameless desperation he went home to the house on Prairie Road. It had been boarded up for several years, but owing perhaps to the strangeness of the events that transpired there, little vandalism was apparent, and no attempts had been made to break in.

And so, Quinn himself broke in and slept on the floor, and when after some weeks no one called the sheriff, he pulled the plywood off the windows, and when still none objected, he repaired the flue and cleaned the stove and built a fire in the grate he was sure the whole valley could see.

And see they did, yet nothing was said, and no neighbor arrived to complain of his presence, nor County official to roust him from his forsaken property. The land and the house were of course no longer his, Quinn having failed to pay taxes for half a decade, and he believed that to be true for several months until one day a fussy looking city fellow knocked on the door and asked Quinn if he was interested in selling the property. Quinn was at a loss for what to say, but being at best a truthful drunk, he stated his ignorance of the land's ownership.

The dude then asked if he were not William Quinn, and

Quinn admitted that he was, at which point the fellow produced a copy of the deed which showed the current owner to be one William R. Quinn. Quinn was aghast, then confused, and he summarily ordered the stranger off his property, which was to be his habit for the next thirty-three years.

That someone had paid Quinn's taxes, in Quinn's name for each of the six preceding years, was the seed of change that slowly began to germinate in the man's impoverished soul. That anyone knowing Quinn, what he had done, could make such a selfless gesture in the face of the moral outrage that infused the community was beyond the ken of the tragic man who had precipitated it. The thought itself became an epiphany, and the deed of the Good Samaritan therefore sacrosanct, enough that Quinn was able to transcend even his own malignant self image such that he allowed himself the chance to become whole again, or at least more whole, possessing at best the barest utility of a man, as much as thumb and forefinger might suffice as a hand.

Though Quinn made no direct inquiries as to the name of his benefactor—as he rarely spoke directly to anyone—he made certain private inquiries at the assessor's office, and from these he learned only that the anonymous donor had paid in cash, thereby concealing his identity and making his philanthropy even more a thing of inexplicable kindness.

That Quinn did not make a greater effort, or a greater show of finding out the donor's identity, struck his detractors as more of Quinn's arrogance, his ingratitude and intractability. Others said he was simply ashamed, as any man would be who accepted such charity.

Will Quinn never worked for or with another man again, and if the seed of his recovery was miraculous the pace of it was not, and it was many years before another logger would look at him and think that Quinn had done well by himself, if not by others.

Quinn kept good faith in his business dealings, but he kept no friends, and a solitary light in one room of his home was all his neighbors saw as they drove by of a twilight evening. He never drank again, but something of his spirit was forever tarnished by his alcoholism, and the house on Prairie Road appeared to reflect that fact. But appearance was all it was, and though as years went by and the house took on a dilapidated look, there was also an underlying order about it, and those who thought they knew Quinn believed they understood: The disheveled appearance of the house was due not to neglect but from a hesitancy on Quinn's part to alter it, as though change would equal another kind of loss, if only the memory of a happier time. And so, the house became a patchwork of minor repairs, which were themselves repaired until the house became a crazy quilt of weathered boards and rusted nails.

One day, some twelve years after the death of Lou Kettle, Quinn left his house and crossed a field, entered a woodlot, and emerged at the door of his closest neighbor. He knocked on the door and another man answered, and both stood silent for some moments, something transpiring in the look they gave each other, and when Quinn eventually extended his hand, the shorter man took it. Neither actually shook the other's hand but squeezed it with a grip like to break the bones of an unwitting, unwary acquaintance. Laying an envelope containing several thousand dollars on the porch rail, Quinn then returned to his debt free home, never having uttered a word.

"So, no one ever knew?" the boy asked. "No one found out who paid the taxes?"

"Some thought they did," said Randall Toffness. "But we ain't all Ruth Hatch around here. Some of us can keep a secret. Nothin' against Ruth, mind you," he quickly added.

"Of course not," Will smiled.

The sun had arced a considerable distance across the sky and their beer cans had been empty the better part of an hour. Solitary cedars in the middle of a field cast elongated shadows on the grass, and grazing cattle began to venture from the hazel coolness of the woods. Redwing blackbirds flitted about on a rusted strand of barbwire, the shocking color of them blending with a row of poppies that bordered the fence line. Will tried to picture where the garden had been, close enough to the road that his grandmother could see the cars go by but distant enough to avoid their scrutiny.

When the white convertible drove past again and honked, Will drifted off in his mind, and though he saw the girls with their long hair blowing, he pictured instead an older, '40s vintage pickup truck with the somber Louisa Kettle in its bed, and tried to imagine the expression on her face, and that of his grandmother as she turned her eyes away.

"Them girls are in deep shit if Len Dockett sees 'em," said Toffness. "He prizes that car more'n his own life. Certainly more'n his daughter's."

Randy smiled to show he was joking, but Will didn't seem to take notice.

"You okay?" Toffness asked in afterthought, having given the young man an earful.

"I'm tired, is all. Haven't slept very much. Still have a long way to go."

"Then how 'bout I give you a lift?"

"It's a long way," said Will. "End of the Suiattle River Road."

"Thirty miles," the old man confirmed. "That ain't nothin'. I've lived here my whole life, driven hours to work and back."

"Well, if you don't mind."

"Mind?" said Toffness. "Hell, I'm retired. Nothin' left to mind. Climb in," he said, and stood with a theatrical groan.

They made a loop of the Prairie Road and Toffness talked the whole time, giving Will the historical perspective of every house, cow, and stump they passed. Beyond town they passed the log yards and the mill, then the Forest Service District Office, and farther down they cruised past the cul-de-sac of identical, vinyl-sided houses that was the modern-day Sauk-Suiattle Reservation. River skiffs on flat bed trailers were parked along the rutted drives, fishing nets draped on carport walls, waiting to be mended. Boned-out pickups and tarp-covered campers sat perched on cinder blocks, an assortment of toddlers' Day-Glo toys littering the hard-packed yards. Small children stared as the red pickup passed, unblinking in the roil of dust.

Rounding a corner near a confluence of rivers, the steel bridge rose before them, pale green against dark green, milk green water passing beneath. Will knew without asking that this was the bridge where his grandmother had jumped to her death, and as the pickup sped across its length the sound of its tires on the steel grid deck issued a wailing sound, reverberant, high pitched as a tuning fork, like something only an animal could hear.

"You know how he died," Toffness said, more a statement than question.

"Drowned," said Will, not meeting his gaze, which he knew was trained on him.

To his credit, the old man didn't slow, but sped on off the bridge toward the Suiattle River turnoff. "He drowned, all right," said Toffness. "That part ain't no lie."

Will waited for Toffness to go on, and when he didn't, said, "Sounds like there's a story in that."

Toffness laughed. "Story about everything around here."

Will felt compelled to ask for that story, but in truth he was disappointed in his pilgrimage, disillusioned of his family's past and the mystery of his heritage. Fact was, he didn't think he liked his grandfather, what he'd learned of him, and was afraid he'd be unmoved by the story of his death. And such a thought, such an ending after all these years, was not one the young man was anxious to accept.

"Maybe another time," said Will. "I need to sort things out."

Toffness was reflective for several minutes, unconsciously fingering his cap, rubbing his bristled jaw. Downshifting then on the uphill grade, he was nodding to himself, Will saw. Randall Toffness was a thoughtful man. A Good Samaritan at heart.

"You'll be back then, sounds like," Toffness said.

"Sure," said Will. "I guess."

It was twenty-three miles of logging road to the Suiattle River trailhead, and for the remainder of the drive the two men talked of lakes and mountains and the journeys they'd taken among them. And yes, Will conceded, he'd have liked it in the old days, the risks men took and the freedoms they'd wrested, some of them abused but much of it exulted in. So much had changed in so short a time, the perception of the endless, rugged country that men like Toffness exploited quickly transformed into finite, precious wilderness that younger men sought to preserve. The mountains were a mystery, and those who lived and journeyed amongst them were complex pieces of its puzzle. With edges rounded, bludgeoned, or frayed, they appeared at times to not fit within it—but all did, in their way. All did.

When they arrived at the trailhead both men got out and stood by the truck for some minutes. It was five, maybe six o'clock by then, and the puffy white clouds of late afternoon leaned like sails before the wind. Will drew on his pack, adjusted its straps, cinched the buckle at his waist. Shaking hands, the younger man squeezed with all his might and the older man grinned with amusement.

"You're gettin' the hang of it," Toffness chuckled.

The boy's smile was genuine as he flexed his fingers in the aftermath of the gesture. "I won't require the hand for some days," he drawled, trying to match the older man's wit.

"Be thankful you've got a whole one," Toffness intoned, the levity gone from his eyes. "It's in men to judge, so I won't tell you not to. But be kind about it. Be kind."

Toffness stood watching as the purple backpack blended into shadow, vanishing at length up the trail. Swinging his boot to the chrome rung of the truck, he pulled his aching body into the cab and headed back toward town. As the miles slipped by and the sunlit shadows of alder and maple flared across the windshield, he relived all the things he'd spoken of that day, right up to the question he'd posed to the boy as they'd crossed the span of the bridge.

He should have made the young Quinn listen. He should have given him something more than the pathetic image of his grandfather: a cruel, uncaring, violent drunk, swept to his death while other men watched.

Almost as Toffness completed the thought, he pulled the truck into a graveled turnout and killed its diesel engine. There he sat gazing across the valley at the alder-choked scar of a very old clearcut. Down in the throat of the narrow canyon the river ran fast and loud, coursing through ladders of sheer rock walls awash with the spray of whitewater. Some thousand feet above it the flat of an old landing could vaguely be discerned, a moldering log deck grown up in willow, lime green in the wash of dark blue. It was all that remained of the winter setting where Quinn had lost his hand. No one would recognize it that hadn't been there, nor have any reason to recall.

Fishing a beer from the Igloo cooler, he held it unopened in his hand, feeling the cold seep into his flesh like it had that storied day. Staring at the folds of timbered mountains that rose toward the shoulders of the unseen volcano, the sunlight was softened in the filigree of treetops, the silver spears of old growth snags gleaming like tapers in the waning rays. The golden light crept sidelong up the valley, met halfway by the hardedge of shadow that moistened the bottomland with mist.

Toffness had watched the seasons change for seventy-some-odd years, and yet he remembered each day that had passed with a clarity born of hard times, frozen like fir needles suspended in a pond, landing fires blazing in the night. He remembered where he was, who he was with, and the words they'd spoken together, as intimate and distinct as observing a hand held in front of one's face. Or half a hand, he remembered now, the thought unbidden though not unwelcome, yet tragic just the same.

The winter of 1991 was much like that of '54. It snowed over Christmas through New Year's Day, right up to the full moon of January when it froze. The stars shone bright over white clad mountains and the temperature dipped toward the teens, then single digits that iced the high lakes, hovering at zero on Saint Valentine's Day.

Traffic was negligible on the county roads, the tinkle of tire chains in the still, frozen air discernable for nearly a quarter mile before any vehicle appeared. The plows had bladed the snow to black ice and there was little to do but sand, light flares, and wait for the car wrecks to occur. Skidder loggers didn't mind so much, as long as they had room to cold deck. Winter sales were lowland shows, and the yarding was easier on frozen ground, negating the nuisance of mud.

Other men prayed for a change in the weather, and when eventually it came they were glad. But relief faded quickly as warm Chinook winds blew hard from the south, gale force tides that knocked down trees and snapped off power poles. At the height of the wind the rain arrived and began to fall in earnest, and within hours the river had crested to flood stage and smaller bridges were quickly lost in the onslaught of rampaging creeks. Freezing levels hovered near eight thousand feet, and the two months of snow washed down the frozen mountains until all that had once been chaste and white turned gray and shades of dark brown. Schools were closed, and the State and County crews worked at night under lights, and there was even talk on the evening news of calling in the National Guard. TV crews were amongst the hordes of rubberneckers who mobbed each bridge about to go under, or road or home imperiled. Hundreds of people in varying colors of raingear interfered with the efforts of flood workers, and fast-thinking foremen tried to organize the curious into sandbaggers. When that failed, State Troopers ticketed the parade of cars and arrested those who were too drunk to drive away.

There was a strange, festive atmosphere throughout the valley, in sharp contrast to the despair felt by those whose homes had been damaged or whose land was in danger of washing away. Some saw it as a chance for quick profit, as was always the case when government money poured into a disaster area, be it flood, forest fire, or windstorm. Any man with a piece of equipment was hired and mobilized by the State, and the creeks and riverbanks were crawling with bulldozers, dump trucks, and track hoes.

Of these William Quinn was one, though not the kind who saw only profit in it. Quinn had done well enough over the years. He was not a rich man by any account, yet he owned his equipment, and his land, and was beholden to few except those who lived only in memory, though to these, in his mind, he was forever indebted.

The years had not been kind to Quinn and in fact were as unkind and abusive as he'd been to himself. There were many deep scores in the planes of his face, severe lines converging at his mouth and eyes that seemed gathered by needle and thread. Though he shaved every morning, his jaw was always gray, his once fine nose grown fleshy and florid with age. There was something in his appearance reminiscent of his home, a disheveled yet faithfully maintained look revealed by a razor knick on the point of his chin, a harsh, blunt cropping of silver hair which he cut without benefit of mirror. He was as clean-shaven and close shorn as he'd been as a teenage choker setter, yet the eyes that stared from the husk of his face told the tale of many long years, many dark hours of solemn grief and morbid introspection that no young man could ever envision for himself.

In the first year of Quinn's return to the Prairie Road he'd cut shake blocks as he always had, but these were legal sales from the Forest Service, and his overhead—a pickup truck and a chainsaw—was low. In another year he'd bought a tired old Cat for five hundred dollars whose tracks and sprockets were worn to nubs. He nursed it along for a few more years then upgraded to a pair of rubber-tired Timberjacks that he cannibalized one from the other for another half decade, salvaging logs from the wasteful devastation of the railroad loggers many years past. The once forsaken logs were straight-grained and sound if you bucked off the punky ends, and they looked as good as any going down the road. Quinn contracted the hauling and paid by the thousand, as he himself was paid.

And so it went for a dozen more years, until he'd garnered enough credit to broker a Link-Belt line machine that could be rigged for both yarding and loading, which nearly killed the now middle-aged man in his adamancy for working alone. His half a hand was hard and polished yet just as pink as the other, thickly calloused on the penumbraed, crescent scar. He worked as hard as he ever had but in ingenious ways to account for his handicap, and many thought this was why he worked alone—so none could see his struggle and take pity on it. But others felt he'd simply become a solitary man, even a lonely one, as if in penance for his sins, or as some still said, his crimes.

And thus, by the winter of '91 Will Quinn owned and worked an orange Koehring track hoe, a state-of-the-art hydraulic shovel with bucket and grapples that could log and load and dig or move anything anywhere. The levered control system was kind to his crippled hand, the cab was heated, and not a single crack appeared in the expensive, polarized windshields.

At the height of the historic flooding that year he and his machine were ferried from creek to creek and bridge to bridge, until by afternoon of a Sunday on the last day of his life, Quinn slowly walked the shovel off the tilt-bed lowboy owned by Randy Toffness, a contract logger and trucker oft employed by Quinn to move his equipment. Once on solid ground, Quinn cocked the boom and swung the house and wasted no time wading into the log jam of uprooted trees that threatened to dam the Sauk River and potentially destroy the bridge that spanned its ever-increasing breadth. It was Violet's bridge; that's how Quinn thought of it every time he crossed, a near-daily experience for the last four decades of his life.

The strategy was identical to that of Pick-Up Sticks, to carefully remove each tree such that others were not dislodged, thereby causing the pile to shift and possibly break up, sending a fusillade of lunkers downriver to strike the bridge. The bridge's concrete pylons were already clogged with debris, the brown water churning around them in curtains of chocolaty foam. The river swept whole trees along in its current, their radiating root-wads the cleverest of battering rams, their naked limbs writhing like so many arms raised in the futility of free fall.

A large crowd was on hand to witness the possible destruction of the bridge, sheltering themselves from the driving rain in anything from raingear to plastic garbage sacks, huddled together in groups, some with children, turning their hooded heads in surprise when thirty-ton dump trucks inched through the crowd laden with loads of riprap. State troopers garbed in yellow slickers and wide-brimmed hats passed amongst them, trying to establish a perimeter but to little avail. Cars and pickups lined the road for a solid mile, and some drove down through the fishing trails to park at the river's edge, licks of wild music audible against the thunderous din of the floodwaters, as though nature had thrown an outrageous party and all had come to partake.

The rain poured down as a continuous diagonal presence, daylight leached from the sky and replaced by an ever-present dusk. By three o'clock the big lights were turned on, banks of a dozen mounted on trucks and powered by diesel generators. There were similar lights on the far side of the bridge, and similar crowds of people, and more machines and double-bellied semis dumping riprap along the shore. On that side as well, for some distance upriver, carloads of young people had driven down the brushy tracks to park on the banks and drink, blinking their headlights and beeping their horns, futilely calling to friends on the other side.

Quinn snaked a full-length hemlock from the logjam and drew it abreast of the machine, swinging the house with its massive counterweight and dragging the tree to its center of balance before him. Snagging it with the grapples at a point less that halfway from the roots, he lifted its weight and engaged one track, and the Koehring pivoted away from the river with the waterlogged tree in tow. Dumping the load, he maneuvered back and grappled another log, the D-9 behind him blading the hemlock onto a mounting pile, clearing the way for Quinn's next turn.

Running the shovel was easy work compared to struggling in the brush, yet it wore Quinn out, the constant jerking of the machine as it rocked on its tracks, the centrifugal physics of the swinging house replicated faithfully in the small of his back. His bad hand ached from fingering the joystick, a slow, incessant, insistent burn like the whickering flame of a candle. Yet William Quinn was accustomed to pain, his only real companion, and he knew no other man of his age and kind who was not well acquainted with it.

He observed the arc lights snap on at mid-span of the bridge, the flashing light bars of the state patrol cruisers as well. The skeletal girders lit up red and blue, strobing in and out of shadow as true dusk rushed toward darkness. The arc lights were focused on the center pylon where the jagged detritus of the storm was piling higher, the muddy water rising in powerful rooster tails like the crashing of surf at the ocean. Men in hard hats and rain gear could be seen at the bridge rail, leaning cautiously to peer over its edge, some with radios in hand.

The bridge, five hundred feet long and forty feet high at its center, was some two hundred yards below Quinn's log jam, and in the fading light and the beating of his windshield wipers it was becoming more difficult to see. Switching on his own lights, the cab and boom-mounted lamps cast an incandescent halo of stark white around the perimeter of the hoe, lending the machine a futuristic, insect-like appearance, its exoskeleton of cleats and hydraulic lines broken in a geometry of black shadow and orange paint, the swiveling house, the jointed arm and articulated pincers of the grapples—much like Quinn's hand, a literal thumb and forefinger—revealed as the near living muscle it was.

Some hundred yards above the logjam a sandy section of undercut riverbank weakened and clove away, and a van full of high school kids tumbled with it into the fast-moving water. Quinn didn't see it happen, but when he swung around with another log a bouncing matrix of flashlight beams appeared to thread the underbrush, and the old cat skinner leaped up on his tracks and rapped on the door of his cab.

Quinn was apprised of the situation, and he and Tottness quickly devised a plan in which Randy would clear a path through the alder such that Quinn could walk the shovel to the calved bank and possibly snag the van before it was swept away.

There were young Indian kids in the van, and at first the eroded bank itself sufficed to hold the vehicle in place, and in those panicked moments some managed to climb from the windows and leap for shore where others leaned with arms extended. But soon the cloven berm was washed from beneath it and the van shifted, then shifted again, and as friends shouted to roll up the windows the van was borne away in the turbulent river and dragged toward the raging crown at its center.

All watched as it bobbed, skidded, stopped and then lurched forward again, pummeled by rocks and uprooted trees, the Earth's own weaponry unleashed by the storm. None could quite believe what they were seeing, and all conviviality was drained from the crowd. The trucks and equipment stopped growling at their work until there was only the resonant rumbling of floodwater and the interminable lashing of rain.

The van tumbled twice in a full 360 then righted itself again, navigating the current much like a boat, but cocked at an angle such that anything could tip it and start it tumbling again. The arc lights on the bridge were trained on its shape as it approached the center pylon, the funnel of luminescence serrated by rain, capturing the plight of the foundering vehicle in its perfectly conical beam. Those at the bridge rail would later say they could see the young faces of those inside, pressed to the windows, their expressions mute, looking not at each other but out at the water that swept them toward certain, unequivocal death.

Quinn heard the shrieking whoop of a siren, observed a police cruiser speeding away as hard hats scattered into action. Swinging open the door of his cab, he squinted into the maelstrom, the arc lights lighting the van's metal roof, now pinned against the tangle of bucking logs that jammed the bridge's pylon.

Sighing, he leaned and spat a stream of snoose to vanish in the driving rain, then looked toward the Nine where Randy stood, gazing solemnly back.

Quinn nodded once to his only friend, closed the door and swung the house, and the Koehring lurched toward the river. Walking it above the shoreline jam, he eased it into deeper water in a blinding geyser of mud, the lights on his cab casting spidery tracers that illumined the frothing wave crests. The water was higher near the bank's concavity, and for some minutes he could not see his tracks as they spun and ground for purchase, and those on shore were heard to remark that the orange house and crab-like arm appeared to be creeping along of themselves. From the depths of what had once been a slow green pool, Quinn finally gained traction and rose above the water such that his tracks became visible again, enough to pilot his way downstream and angle cautiously across, making his way toward the river's center in a nerve-racking process of pivot and heel. Waves breached the cab in backlit fantails of gravelly brown translucence, rocks and trees deadheading the counterweight which Quinn kept angled upstream, the boom extended in the opposite direction, knuckling into the raging current to provide some modicum of balance.

Debris tore at the boom and grapple hoses, and through the bright lights Quinn discerned arcs of hydraulic fluid spuming out under pressure. He could feel but not hear the grating of the tracks and imagined the boulders tearing at the belly pan, the drive sprockets pulverized by the continuous impact of pile driving, waterborne missiles.

All watched as the track hoe braved the insurgence of angry, unbridled nature, its progress slow but unrelenting, its occupant ensconced in its tiny cab in that casual attitude of nonchalance that all operators unwittingly assumed. At the base of the pylon the van teetered in the grip of the logjam, shuddering with the impact of each projectile thrown against it. A rainbow of colored ropes dangled above it, draped from the bridge deck where the blue, red, and amber lights of ambulances, squad cars, and mountain rescue teams swirled against the now total darkness. Men in climbing gear stood ready at the rail, clipped into their ropes but waiting, perhaps for an order or even a reason to descend, as there was nothing they could do unless the track hoe succeeded in reaching the pylon, and if the man inside it did not himself require rescue.

With each rogue swell that broke over Quinn's cab the bank-side crowds gasped in concert, as well as with every shift of the logjam that battered the van and its cargo of terrified teenagers. The Deputies called to the kids on their bullhorns, and expecting no response, received none. None could imagine the scene inside the van, the injuries, the hysteria, the absolute terror of being trapped in close proximity to death.

Quinn had closed to within a hundred feet of the bridge when he felt the Koehring slide. Correcting course with a shift of the boom, he pivoted in lead with the water's force, knowing he'd need to crab again to maintain a diagonal with the logjam. In the midst of the process, the forty-ton shovel was rocked and shoved hard a second time. He resolved to back up and regain his trajectory, which he succeeded in doing by retracting the arm, planting it, paying it out again as the engine struggled to pull the weight of the machine against the growing strength of the river.

The spectators on the bridge and riverbanks cheered when they saw what Quinn had done, giddy with excitement and a tempered trepidation, exulting in any opportunity for hope. Quinn eased to within a boom's length of the logjam, and when his lights swept the van he saw a face, the quiescent features of an Indian girl briefly illuminated in a window. It was there for a moment, then as quickly gone, and Quinn went doggedly about his work, jockeying for some semblance of stability, dipping into the morass of splintered wood that pinned the van on the upstream side, threatening to crush it and all those inside. These trees he grappled and drew carefully out, swinging around quickly, releasing them into the muddy brown water that swept everything into darkness.

He worked cautiously, steadily, with the same expertise he'd always exhibited in his efforts, no matter what they were or whom they benefited, if any. When he swung the house to release his catch, the solid steel counterweight no longer at his back, the cab was exposed to the tons of debris that sluiced headlong downriver, and the machine rocked mightily with the impact of each projectile, one track lifting at angles to the blow. The pile shifted suddenly, and the van began to roll—to the dramatic gasping of the crowd—and he quickly cribbed it up again with the same poles and treetops that once had pinned it.

Above him, two tow trucks backed to the bridge rail and their winch lines began to unspool. From one line dangled a metal cage in which a man might stand; the other, perhaps some ten feet removed, held only a grappling hook. Glancing up at their progress as he worked, Quinn divined their intent, devising his own part in it. In his mind, if not in the window of the van, he saw the face of the Indian girl, her broad, flat features, long dark hair, the implacable calm in her eyes. He knew in that moment that she would survive and he would perish in her stead, and the sudden acceptance felt natural as rain, as warm and replenishing as sunshine.

Even as he absorbed the thought, the battered van lurched sideways, rolling, nearly tumbling in its bid to rush past him. With unthinking skill his hands moved on the joy sticks and the grapples snapped out and grabbed it; walking the Koehring abreast of the wreckage, he wedged the van tight to the pylon.

From his vantage point beneath the bridge, the glare of the lights was diced in squares by the open steel grid of the deck, ribbed in black lines by the matrix of girders, broken in checkerboard patterns. Half the Koehring's lights were smashed out, and Quinn could feel the declining pressure as the leaking hydraulics bled off.

The shapes of two men appeared in silhouette dangling above the river. One reached out and grabbed hold of the line from which the steel hook swiveled, the other shouting into a handheld mic to those leaning over the rail, his words sucked away in the roar of the river and the boulders scouring its bottom.

The top of the van was crushed against the pylon, the Koehring's track snugged to its chassis, the broken windows on the passenger's side beginning to take on water. The efforts of the men who dangled from the ropes were futile, Quinn could see. There was no way of reaching the van where it lay, no chance to secure it with the hook.

Many men who work in the woods like to boast of their prowess with equipment, priding themselves in the skill and speed with which they could load a truck, lay a grade, or feather a turn of logs. Quinn was not one of them. He worked alone and his deeds went unheralded, and he was generally unimpressed with himself. But he was possessed of a mechanical facility that could only be described as extraordinary, perhaps due the likeness of the Koehring's steel claw and his own misshapen hand, an affinity of purpose and mindless utility that melded flesh and throbbing machine in a tactile sensitivity similar to, or best imagined as, the pain one feels in missing limbs long since amputated.

Thus, when Quinn raised the Koehring's boom it was like his own arm reaching, and when the grapples snagged the bight of the cable it was his clawed hand, and when the jiggle of one scarred finger on the joystick hooked the van's undercarriage it was like the ghost of all his long-denied decency reaching out across time and travail to converge in a single act, crushing his fate in a hardy handshake that brought literal tears to his eyes.

When the man on the rope spoke into his radio the winch line drew instantly taught. The van jerked once, its axle secured, and slowly rose clear of the river, brown water sluicing from its shattered windows, cheers thundering like rain from above. Then the hurtling shape of a monstrous root wad eclipsed the glaring light, the negative image of a radiant sun that rushed up at Quinn and sheered the Koehring's house completely off its carriage, sweeping it downriver like a cow on the tracks where the next day the orange cab was recovered with Quinn's body still in it, down around the bend of the river where Violet was found those many years before.

It was close to dusk when Randall Toffness walked into the Hang Up Tavern, the screen door banging behind him, the lemony hint of a startling sunset reflected in storefronts across the street. It was muggy inside, the humidity of the day slow in escaping. Most of the tavern's lights were switched off to detract from the oppressive heat, the neon beer signs that blinked in the windows lending a melancholic glow.

Ruth Hatch, showered and primped for night shift, pulled a draught for Toffness and set it before him on a cardboard coaster. Nodding his thanks, he quaffed the beer's head while Ruth stood impatiently by, her red painted fingernails drumming the bar. Wiping the foam from his upper lip, Toffness said nothing, and when he only sat nodding with his hairy arms folded, Ruth fairly shouted, "For goodness' sake Randy, what happened?"

Other heads at the bar then turned to hear, their feigned disinterest quickly cast off like itchy black woolies come spring. Everyone knew of Quinn's grandson's arrival and, like small-town folk everywhere, felt it their due to be appraised of his welfare.

Toffness took another sip of beer, replaced the glass on the coaster, and speaking directly to Ruth as though no one else was listening, said, "Nothin'."

"Nothing? Didn't you talk to him?" Ruth asked, knowing full well that he had, having heard from Len Dockett, who was having a helluva time with that teenaged daughter of his.

"Sure," said Toffness, "we spoke."

"That's all?" said Ruth.

"We had us a beer," Toffness elaborated. "Then I gave him a ride."

"He's gone?" said Ruth, her dismay, even shock, apparent in her penciled eyebrows. "Where'd he go?"

"Back to the hills," said Toffness, then turning to the others, the other men and wives who'd known Will Quinn all their lives, added, "He's a good kid. A decent young man."

"So you told him?" said Ruth.

"I told him about his grandfather, his grandmother. All I knew, as I knew it."

Some at the bar turned slowly away, appearing to study their schooners.

"How'd he take it?" Ruth asked.

"Like a man," Toffness chuckled, and tossed back a great draught of beer.

"Ohh," moaned Ruth. "Ohh," she repeated, wringing the bar rag in her hands. "I feel so sorry for that boy. He seemed so . . . happy, I guess."

"Nothin' to pity," said Toffness. "The boy sought the truth, and he got it."

"So you told him the ending? You told how he died?"

Ruth stood pensive on her side of the bar, bent at her aproned waist, her false eyelashes narrowed for a good, long squint at a suddenly recalcitrant Randy Toffness.

"You didn't tell him!" Ruth shrieked, aghast, quickly becoming indignant. "You didn't tell how his grandpa died a hero?"

"He didn't want to know," Toffness pleaded. "I offered to tell him. I tried, but . . . it was too much telling at once, I s'pose. But he'll be back," he assured the bar's patrons. "We'll see young Quinn again."

"Oh, Randy!" cried Ruth. "Oh Randy!" she repeated. "You . . . you're dumb as a stump sometimes! He came here looking for something good, and what did you give him? Something terrible is what! Something awful!"

All at the bar then looked away, solemn at the occasion of Ruth Hatch's tongue lashing of poor old Randall Toffness.

"Why . . ." said Ruth, "if that boy never comes back . . ." And a look of sudden, implacable resolve nearly cracked the facade of her freshly rouged face.

"I'm gonna write him a letter," she said, throwing the towel on the bar. Pivoting smartly on her orthopedic heel, she headed back toward the kitchen.

"Pour me another before you go!" Toffness called after her, and Ruth called back, as she slipped through the swinging doors, "Pour it your damn self, you silly old fool! You ain't that retired!"

When Ruth returned she held a clipboard full of old receipts and scrap paper she'd saved for just such a purpose, and taking a seat at the end of the bar, far away from her customers, she pulled a pen from behind her ear.

"You don't even have an address," shouted Toffness.

"I do too," said Ruth. "His daddy's at the university, down there in Eugene. I'll get off a letter to him."

And so Ruth began, scratching in green ink in her loopy cursive on the back of a bill for a dozen kegs of Oly. Dear William, she began. You may not remember me, Ruth Hatch, from way up here in little old . . .

A moment later she stopped, the pen poised thoughtfully at her ruby red lips, and sat motionless, helpless, staring at the ceiling.

S ome six miles up the trail from where Toffness had left him, Will Quinn made camp in a stand of giant cedars, by the side of the river where he could listen to its voice. He unrolled his bivvy sack and spread his sleeping bag to loft, then gathered wood for a fire. The fire itself was only for company, and on his camp stove he cooked a quick meal: Minute Rice, a handful of dried vegetables, a plastic packet of soy sauce.

It had been a hard twelve hours for young Quinn. There were rugged mountains he'd rather have climbed than to realize the truths he'd learned that day. He felt bereft of something, something he'd never actually had but which had long been promised, something that had always held promise: a sense of belonging to a place and a lineage rooted in the mountains that he loved.

Will did not remember his mom. She'd died when he was very young, younger even than his father had been when he'd lost his own mother. There wasn't even a floral print dress to remind the boy of his loss, nor the color of her hair, or the strong smell of soap that his father described when speaking of Violet. William Quinn Junior had never remarried, and with his young son had moved from town to town, university to university, until they ended up in Eugene, renting a small house where Will's father still lived, in a part of the city soon swallowed by development until it was surrounded by gas stations, minimarts, and the incessant hum of human traffic.

Will pictured his father as the young boy from Toffness's story, wrapped in blankets in the flag-fluttering chicken coop, shivering with cold and fear. With the images of death still fresh in his mind, he'd heard his drunken father arrive in the night, but even then chose to stay hidden, safe within the confines of his mother's odd shrine. Then hearing the gun shot that ended the life of the speckled bitch, perhaps seeing Quinn drag the carcass through the snow with his terrible hook of a hand.

That Will Quinn had never left the safety of the coop. He would always remain inside it, wrapped in his blanket of books and ideas and the courageous lives of others, his desk by the window offering only a view of a yard, a fence, and other inward-looking windows, nothing like the view that even the pathetic elder Quinn could enjoy from the house on the Prairie Road. At least Will knew the reason for it now, though he'd return to his father empty handed, bringing nothing to release the man from his fear, no word of the good deeds Quinn might have done after having destroyed his family. Even in death he was destroying it still, his son still waiting for his mother to save him, as Violet sought salvation from another. And that sad man, now gone to his maker, had failed even at saving himself.

Exhausted both physically and emotionally, Will's Spartan meal did nothing to fill the void he felt inside himself, in no way assuaging the craving he'd felt from the moment he'd entered the valley of his family's past. It was too hot to crawl into his sleeping bag, and so he lay atop it, the fire painting an orange blush on the bower of surrounding trees. Within the fire the coals glowed hot and forms took shape in their midst, the silhouette of a dog, a bear's savage maw, a human face in profile. Eons later the smoke turned blue and a log crumbled down into coals, a single spark rising to vanish into darkness, the wink of a star through the trees. The firelight sifted through the over-hanging limbs, swaying in the evening's breeze, the shadow and substance of graceful boughs passing as if between worlds. Try as he might he could not discern shade from transient twig, the trembling of each and the flickering light creating a netherworld of choices, of perceptions, and belief.

Closing his eyes upon that koan, the sound of the river rushed in, the voices within it palpable, nearly discernable. In Hesse's Siddhartha the river had spoken to Gautama Buddha, imparting its ancient wisdom. Will always thought of water that way, as a voice, the voice of the wilderness that whispered its secrets to all with the patience to listen. He'd learned from his reading that Indians had inhabited the North Cascades since the end of the Ice Age, some ten thousand years past. Will wondered if the ancestors of Louisa Kettle had traveled to this same spot, building a campfire and dreaming around it with the same orange puzzle of cedar boughs and slow-moving images in the coals, the voice of the river speaking a language they could sense but never decipher.

Will was just nodding off to these thoughts when first he heard the sound, a rustling of branches as of something large moving through the brush. He was on his feet in a second, standing with his back to the fire, staring intently at the total darkness of the forest, made even blacker, more intangible by the orange wicker of flame. The rustling noise moved slowly around him, just beyond the circumference of light, a patient, curious circle of predation with young Will posed at its center.

All thoughts of the past, all images of ancestors both ancient and contemporary were instantly vanquished by the immediacy of the present, and Will's mind snapped to that heightened awareness usually reserved for the spines of mountains and the focus required to scale them. Without benefit of sight his senses were attuned solely to his hearing, and every popping coal and trickle of water was winnowed and isolated from this other sound that took such sudden precedence. Whatever was out there was big, Will discerned, confident and lumbering and unconcerned with stealth beyond the condition of remaining unseen, if not undetected. But in his mind he did see it: the lanky, emaciated winter bear that slew the unwitting pups, that woofed and snapped and lunged at Violet, falling only after the rifle was emptied, its echoes absorbed by the timber. It was not that bear, though Will saw it as such, convinced as he was that the invisible presence was indeed a bear and not a deer, or coyote, or other forest denizen drawn to the smoke from his fire.

Building the fire higher, he expanded its halo of luminescence and the paltry extent of his vision, but the creature merely retreated from the light and continued its methodical orbit.

Will lost count of the bear's revolutions of his camp; so intent was he on the sounds it made he ceased to turn with it in its meandering ellipse and, kneeling on his sleeping bag, stared only at his shadow where it danced against the timber. Tracking the animal in some part of his mind, it moved around him like the hands of a clock in pursuit of some notion of passage, outside of time and the construct of years by which men measured their lives. Weary, transported, he closed his eyes to all but the sense of its presence, the fire at his back losing brilliance and heat until only the coals remained, the darkness so complete and his exhaustion so profound he no longer knew if his eyes were closed or whether some veil had descended.

Within that state of absolute stillness, his consciousness fluttered like the leaves of a tree, and the images from the stories he'd heard that day, the memories of a past he had only imagined, became lost within each other, superimposed upon themselves until no version was more or less real than another, and the ease of their merging eclipsed even the need to differentiate between them.

He understood that his life and the world in which it transpired were of his own making, and did not result from his past, or the past of others, but was one eternal present amidst other such presents, and that his perception of the world at that very moment was neither the branch nor shadow of the woods his grandfather knew, but was totally his own creation, and the assumptions men made based upon the perceived, evanescent qualities that separated the real from the fantastic were choices, not truths, and were woven together with such unknowing care as to form the very fabric of their lives.

Will cried for some minutes and, in the depth of such emotion, found something that was not like release but abatement, if not like comprehension then acknowledgment, if not like forgiveness then acceptance of the ways of men not like himself, even if he was born of them.

Quinn had loved these mountains, these woods. Will had sensed that even in the terrible portrait painted of him by his only friend, a man hesitant to even call himself that. Whatever voice had spoken to Quinn need not be the one that spoke to others, not the one Will heard, or the Indians who'd camped by this river. The woods belonged to no white man or Indian or any of those who passed within it. Rather, those passersby belonged to it, not in ownership but membership—kinship, more the truth. All was one within its borders, and its borders extended to within its adherents, felt there as the thing called Wilderness.

The voice of the wilderness is not a human one, Will decided. It was just that simple. Whatever men received of its message was their own interpretation, and Quinn's interpretation, though at times beautiful, quixotic, enchanted, was in the end a tragic one but as much a part of nature as a carcass washed ashore, a great snag tumbled in the forest. Will could not blame the woods for his grandfather's deeds, and in the end, he could not blame his grandfather.

If the boy needed heritage, he would take it from such women as Violet Quinn and Louisa Kettle, and from men like Randall Toffness, whose heart was good and whose kindness extended over forty-odd years to be offered as the hope of forgiveness to a boy he'd never met before.

Forgiveness was a funny thing, thought Will, offered as a

gift or withheld as punishment— another of the things men believed they owned, when in truth they were one of its parts.

Somewhere in the depth and darkness of these thoughts, the unseen bear he'd conjured from fear stopped circling and came straight toward him, and with seeing eyes neither closed nor opened, Will watched it come and raised his hand not in defense but in welcome, and the hand he raised was the hooked hand of his grandfather, and the spirit in which he offered it was that of his grandmother, and when the spectral creature opened wide its radiant mouth there flowed from it the sound of a river, and as he slipped between worlds as corporal and transitory as shadow and firelight, the voice of the wilderness whispered in his ear, revealing with a clarity he could not have imagined the answers to questions he would never have dreamed.

Soldier of Fortunes

Marsh dumped his battered corks and rain gear into the bed of his pickup, tossed in his hardhat as an afterthought, and slumped behind the wheel with a sigh. His ratty old gloves were sopping wet from a snow squall late in the day, and he tossed them on the floor by the heater vent to dry out over the weekend. The thumb of one glove was bright red with blood, and he stubbed that finger on the gear shift knob, precipitating an outburst of thumb-sucking rage. "If one mo' nathty thing happenth to me, I'm jus' gonna fucking kill mythelf!" he ranted, swearing like a logger, which was okay, because that's what he was.

Turning the Datsun off Cornell Creek Road, he headed up the Mt. Baker Highway doing forty miles an hour for half a mile before pulling over by the swaybacked, one-hundred-year-old clapboard building that housed the library/post office in the heart of downtown Glacier. A stone's toss away stood Graham's Restaurant/Store, perhaps even older than the library, wood smoke drifting from its crooked stove pipe and into the frosty spring air. Across the two-lane highway, sloping gently toward the river, the mossy roofs of equally old houses rose above the blackberry cane, yet more stovepipes perfuming the air, wreathing the town in a shawl of pale blue. Beyond the rooftops there were only trees and the hum of rushing water, the white mantled crest of a massive volcano just now poking through the clouds.

Marshall ascended the post office steps in a single athletic hop and squeezed into the narrow, closet-sized enclosure that housed the town's few dozen PO boxes. His box was never locked, the barrel having been craftily removed, and through its small window he spied the edge of a powder blue envelope. Plucking it out he instantly recognized Beth Ann's neat penmanship, floral and precise as a wildflower, and after some brief yet anguished reflection he stuffed it in the pocket of his riggin' shirt and dashed back to his idling truck. Spinning gravel back onto the highway, he sped to the only other corner in town where he hung a hard left and coasted to the last and only house on the block.

Esther stood waiting on the sagging front porch, rising on tiptoe when she saw him. Tall and thin and "eleven-and-one-half years old", she wore spotless white sneakers with rainbow laces, red jeans pegged at the ankles, and a hot pink cardigan sweater. Her sky-blue top—a birthday gift from Marshall—was polka-dotted rather gruesomely with a dozen little floating heads of her hero, Michael Jackson. Waving effusively, she smiled with the silvery glint of braces, her blue and blonde Scandinavian features beaming out like sun through honey.

"Hi Marshall!" she sang, lunging into the passenger seat.

"Hi, Ess. What's new?"

"Nothing," she replied, still grinning.

Esther always said nothing; all kids do, Marshall reflected, grinding gears until he found the right one, then tearing around the block to the highway.

Just beyond the library/post office, across from Jim Cannon's and next to Miner Bill's old trailer, they passed Beth Ann's little house, her green-and-white Volkswagen Bug parked sideways in the muddy drive, both its doors open and suitcases strewn around it. The door to the house stood open as well, and Esther, hanging most of her torso out the Datsun's window, shouted with adolescent enthusiasm, "Hi, Beth Ann!" But no head poked from the door to answer, and Marsh sped off out of town.

They were headed for Bellingham, thirty-five miles west, on what had become a fairly ritual bi-monthly excursion to cash a paycheck, eat at a restaurant, and maybe check out a movie. It always happened like this: Marshall dropped off at his truck by the crummy, Esther dropped off by the school bus, and within ten minutes, at around four o'clock, they were headed off into literal sunset toward what sufficed as The Big City.

"You're pretty quiet today," Esther observed, when after a mile Marshall hadn't asked How's school? How's your mom? Or, How's that kid, Richie what's-his-name?

"Tired, I guess," he replied.

"You're always tired, like what else is new. You're just sad over Beth Ann."

"I am not mad."

"I said sad, not mad. Sad!" she corrected, her eyebrows arching for affect.

"Maybe," he answered. "A little."

"You are," she assured him, always one to inform other people of their feelings.

Marshall responded with a capitulating shrug, offered a half-hearted smile.

"How's school?" he asked after a moment's silence.

"It's okay," she said, another form of nothing.

"Learn anything new?"

"Nah."

"C'mon, nothing?"

"Geometry," she conceded.

"Geometry, really? I thought they taught that in high school."

"I'm doing the ninth grade textbook," she explained. "It's easy. It's stupid."

"Humph," Marshall mumbled, easily convinced of his own stupidity, and drove on into glorious sunset.

Esther punched at the radio button and "Thriller" exploded from the speakers. Releasing a high-pitched squeal of delight, she wiggled her bottom on the worn-out seat, fingers snapping, toes tapping, belting it out with a feigned maturity to her voice, "Doo-doo, dot-dot. Thrillaaaah! In! The! Night!"

"Jeez!" she blurted in the middle of Vincent Price, pointing at the bloody glove on the floor mat. "What happened?" she asked, reaching for Marshall's hand.

Drawing it back instinctively, he quickly relented and held up his thumb for inspection. A deep ragged groove ran across its knob and down to the first grimy joint. "Jagger," he explained, and wiggled it around.

"Ick!" she winced. "It looks terrible! What's a jagger?"

"An emaciated, middle-aged rock star from England."

"C'mon, really,"

"It's a broken strand of steel on a cable, like a barb. Makes it more challenging to set chokers."

"You should wash it," she advised. "With hydrogen peroxide, like Beth Ann always does."

Marshall flinched at the mention of Beth's name, recalling the saga of her broken toe. Someone at the bar had knocked over a stool and it fell on and crushed her big toe. She lost the nail eventually, and was always washing that toe with peroxide, bent over in the bathtub, daubing it with a seemingly endless supply of cotton swabs. Beth Ann had discovered hydrogen peroxide like Columbus discovered America.

"I will, Ess, when we get to town."

"It's really gross," she availed him. "In fact, your whole body is ugly. I mean, your arms are all covered with scabs and stuff, your face is scratched, your finger nails are—"

"Hey!" Marsh shouted. "Do I take this shit from an eleven-and-half-year-old kid? No, I do not! So lighten up, will ya? Huh, iron mouth? How do you like that?"

"Okay, Marshall, be an asshole."

"I know," he said, raising his voice, "that your mom would not appreciate that language, so don't go swearing just because I do!"

Marshall's thumb ached, throbbed, reminding him, like a string tied around a finger, that life hurts, that joy comes and goes like the passage of seasons, like leaves turning gold in the fall. Esther, too, had turned morose, sulking over Marshall's outburst, and she turned away and stared out the window. They'd just negotiated the long curve past the Highway 9 cutoff where the valley broadened and the flatlands began. Tulips and daffodils appeared in the yards of tidy roadside homes, forsythia blooming, crocuses croking, as spring made its way up the mountain. Just beyond a border of cottonwood trees, the Nooksack River meandered beside them, the pink and gold colors of the westering sun reflected on its undulant surface.

"It's pretty," said Esther, never one to sulk for long. "It's like driving into a painting, or a movie."

"Yeah," agreed Marshall, "and we're the stars of the film, Esther Von Silvergrin and Marshall Thumblood. A situation comedy with poignant social overtones."

"Or a video," said Esther, "with you and me dancing in the bed of your truck, an invisible singer behind the wheel wearing only your hardhat and one bloody glove."

"Empty-vee. Get it?" Marsh chuckled, goofing on the TV channel, but Esther just rolled her eyes.

Squirming to reach into his back pocket, Marshall pulled out his pouch of tobacco and tossed it in Esther's lap. "Here," he said, "let's see if you're mature and dexterous enough to roll me a cigarette."

Grinning, Esther tore into the pouch with exaggerated relish, and Marsh took the opportunity to turn the radio down a notch. Licking crusted blood from his thumb, wiping it on his sleeve, he asked, "So how's your mom?"

"She's okay," said Esther, struggling with the crinkly Zig Zag papers.

"C'mon, Ess, can't you elaborate a little?"

"She's fine Marshall, what else can I say! Damn!" she grumbled as her tongue licked the cigarette cleanly in two. Glancing at Marshall, expecting rebuke, he instead chose to let the curse slide.

"So how's Earl?" he asked. "Does your mom still see Earl?"

"Yeah. Earl's fine."

"He's okay, you mean?"

"Yeah, Earl's okay. He stays at our house when he's not away fishing. I like Earl. He thinks I'm a good cook."

"Get out!" Marshall gasped. "He likes your cooking, the creator of tomato brownies, pioneer of artichoke hearts and peanut butter, drinker of the brackish juice of olives?"

Unperturbed, twisting at another cigarette, Esther said, "I made him queesh the other night. I helped my mom, and Earl said it was delicious. We used the The Joy of Cooking and I mixed all the ingredients, which is the most important part. Here," she said, and offered Marshall a lumpy yet not too ragged cigarette.

"Hey, that's pretty good."

"I roll excellent cigarettes," she said, punching in the lighter.

"I suppose you roll cigarettes all the time."

"I roll joints."

"Joints? You roll joints?"

"For Earl!" she exclaimed. "He lets me roll them. So what?" she added, having read the look on Marsh's face, who had just flashed on the time when he and Faye, Esther's mom, had come home from a date and found Esther stoned on pot brownies. It happened around the same time as the tomato brownies and Esther's foray into the world of real cooking; too many brownie tins strewn around the kitchen, and the poor kid got totally smashed. Marshall had to hit the hay, but Faye stayed up with her daughter until dawn. Esther had said some pretty strange things that night, things that shook her mom to her core, and after that what weed they had was kept hidden outside in the woodshed.

"Sounds like your mom is really changing," said Marshall.

"Yeah, she's pretty nice to live with these days. And I really do like Earl."

"Good," he decided, and meant it.

Marshall had lived with Esther and her mom for five years, from the time Essie was four until she was almost ten. In the year or two since their breakup, Marshall and Faye had settled into a peaceful detente; they smiled and chatted amicably, respecting a distance, and Marshall was invited to share as much time with Esther as he wanted. Marsh and Esther got along better, too, finally able to appreciate each other in the absence of external conflict. Truth was, Marshall had feelings of guilt about Esther, all of those "if only" ironies applying, and he wondered at times if she ever felt it and perhaps resented him for it. He hoped not, because he really did love her and didn't want his renewed attention to be interpreted as contrition.

"You roll a fine cigarillo," he said when the lighter popped out. "Muchas gracias."

Beth Ann, at twenty-four, was nine years younger than Marshall. Lanky and tall—almost as tall as he was—she had long, expressive, elegant fingers and feet she felt were too big. She too rolled a fine cigarette, much practiced at it, as the state of the ashtrays strewn around her kitchen attested. "I'm gonna quit soon," she'd sworn on many occasions, none of her promises earnest enough to prevent Marshall, who'd quit smoking for almost half a decade, from slipping back into the habit.

Beth's face as she rolled a cigarette, poured a cup of coffee, scribbled in her notebook, was a study in perfection for Marshall, who clandestinely observed her from across the bar, countertop, or campfire, her dark head lowered with feather-soft curls that almost concealed her blue eyes, long eyelashes even more pronounced when viewed from such an angle. The plane of her cheeks, her ski-jump nose, the pout of her lower lip combined in a symmetry fearful enough to make a tiger jealous, broken only by a single, wayward tooth that leaned in her winsome smile.

Though absorbed in the myriad things she did, Beth's attention to each was undivided. From making Kahlua to writing a play to cutting the sleeves off a sweatshirt, Beth almost never just sat there, and as a result of this constant activity, and because her mind was always one step ahead of her body, she continually crushed toes into firewood, elbows onto countertops, fingers in refrigerator doors. And now Marsh wondered if he was just one of those things that Beth had bumped into, a table leg, stair tread, or other form of inanimate object to collide with in her harried voyage from A to B. Only this time she was not the only one to say ouch! Marsh hadn't tried to get in her way, hadn't placed himself in her path; at least he didn't think he had. He'd just been so intrigued by her multitude of interests, from the trivial to the all-important, that he couldn't discern the difference in scale between Beth's rolling a millionth cigarette or applying to graduate school. Because Beth Ann was a student, a student of life, though she preferred to view herself as the academic type, inclined toward a world of libraries and clock towers and the kind of otherwise unobtainable discipline such traditions were supposed to instill.

And therein, he thought, lay the crux of their problem: Beth Ann felt herself to be a transient in the tiny town of Glacier, destined to move on to bigger and better things once her sabbatical there had ended. And Marsh, and Glacier, were indeed something Beth had tripped over, something she had fallen in love with that didn't fit in with the life she'd planned for herself. Marshall now wanted to kiss her sore toe, her bruised shin, because he loved her so much and couldn't bear to see her struggle, to not be smiling, laughing, loving him back. But it was killing him, crushing him, hurting like leg cramps, like steel ripping flesh. But hell, he knew that was part of the job—all was fair in love and logging.

"Shit," he sighed, decelerating for the turn into the log yard and the shop.

"What?" said Esther.

"Nothing" he mumbled, adopting her tactic.

"Argh," she growled, "I hate when grownups do that, like kids can't understand. It's really condescending."

Marsh had to smile, half amused, half amazed, and kept on grinning as he downshifted through the gravel lot. The little Datsun disappeared amidst the concentration of flatbeds, log trucks, and heavy equipment that clogged the shop grounds. The collapsed tube of a yarder poked from the maw of the shop doors, and an old line shovel, its rusty grapples clawed into the hard-packed earth, leaned at angles on a broken track. Marshall's crew bus and the crummy from Side 2 sat idling amidst the throng of grubby loggers, all of them waving paychecks and laughing like hyenas, jawing about hunting, fishing, drinking, the usual things a guy will do on the weekend.

"Hmm," said Esther, "why do you all wear those uniforms?"

"Uniforms?" said Marsh.

"The red suspenders and too-short pants. Those pinstriped shirts, like yours."

"Riggin' shirts," Marshall explained. "They last forever, and you stag your pants so they don't snag a limb, impeding one's speedy escape. And suspenders come in lots of colors, not just red."

"But yours are. Red."

"I'll be right back," he mumbled, unfolding himself from the cab. "I'll leave the truck running with the radio on, so don't drive off somewhere."

They both faked a laugh at his little joke, and Marsh made his way through the crowd toward the office, shaking hands and slapping backs, snapping suspenders as he went. He bummed a chew of Copenhagen from Vic, the accountant, both of them leaning to spit out the door as they discussed insurance benefits, and Marsh noticed Esther across the dusty lot, wriggling around in the cab of the Datsun. She was dancing and singing to a song on the radio, totally absorbed in her young girl's life, oblivious to the massive manifestations of Marshall's own world that loomed overlarge all around her. And in the midst of Vic's explanation of benefits, Marshall thought of Beth Ann, how her world, to him, now seemed as distant and encapsulated as the dashboard environment of his pickup.

Beth's greatest pain and cherished form of anguish was the struggle of women for equality. Nothing hurt her more, or inspired in her more rage or brilliance or the purest kind of excitement. Marshall was no stranger to women, having grown up surrounded by them after the death of his father, the males in his family outnumbered four to one by the so-called fairer sex. He'd loved and been loved by women all his life, and simply could not think of himself as any kind of oppressor. But Beth's outright anger and impassioned resentment had shocked Marshall into the discovery of many deeply held—and even not-so-deeply held—masculine traits that seemed indeed to be the result of a kind of societal brainwashing in which sexual roles were adopted as blithely and unquestioningly as the acceptance of gravity. And he found himself to be possessed of certain gender-specific characteristics that, upon closer examination, he could not believe were his own.

Certainly he was in the heart of it now. There was nothing more male than a logger, nothing more masculine than logging.

"You want this?" said Vic, waving the paycheck in Marshall's face, bringing him back to the present.

"Why not?" Marsh grinned, stuffing the check in his pocket. "As if the pleasure of logging were not enough."

Esther studied the trashed-out interior of the smelly truck, the mud-encrusted floor mats, balled up candy wrappers, saw files and one bloody glove. It was so Marshall, so Glacier, so everything she'd known for as long as she could remember. She supposed she liked her small town life, or she certainly didn't hate it. Her friends at school had fancy cars and big houses farther down the valley, had mothers and fathers, and swings in their yard; one even had a pool. Not that Esther really cared; she'd much rather swim in a mountain lake, a freezing cold tarn, as Marshall would call it, made by a massive old glacier. Marsh knew the names of all the big mountains and had climbed to the top of most, including the biggest, Mountain Baker, where steam drifted up like a flag. A long time ago, when the Earth was young, lava shot out of the ground. It could happen again, and actually did, at another volcano down south. Marsh wasn't afraid, and neither was Esther. They both kind of laughed at the thought.

One time, by a campfire up at Keep Kool, they roasted marshmallows on sticks. But not with the chocolate, which her mom didn't like 'cause it kept Essie up all night! She'd fallen asleep when the fire burned down, and Marsh tucked her sleeping bag around her. She woke up once when the stars were out and heard her mom's tent fly unzip; Faye crouched in the meadow taking a pee, naked in the light of the moon, and Esther stared at her mother's full breasts, reaching up to measure her own. When would that happen? How could it be that someday she'd be just like her mom—grown up, grown out, and sharing a tent with an equally naked man? Not that she thought a great deal of such things, but high on a mountain the world felt much bigger, and dreams of the future nearer.

Some of the candy wrappers were hers from the last time they went to town: M&Ms, Mounds, and Baby Ruths; the Snickers and Rolos were Marshall's. Didn't he ever clean his truck? She laughed, because the answer was no. Marshall kept everything just as it was, the same as the time before. If Beth went away his whole world would change, like driving his truck through a car wash, familiar but different, less than it was before all the mud was hosed off.

Staring at Marshall's blood-stained glove, she kicked it away with her toe, then pinched its stiff cuff between pink lacquered fingers and tossed it under the seat. She still knew it was there, it would not disappear, but at least she could start to ignore it. Eventually everything went away if kept out of sight long enough. That's what her mother always did, and Esther adopted the habit. Marshall had left the glove right in plain view; he'd probably wear it again! She was sure that he would, and no matter how gross, the thought made her happy somehow. Sometimes it was good when things stayed the same. There was no way to tell until after.

Back in the truck, turning down the radio, Marshall asked, "What was that song you were dancing to?"

"What song?" said Esther.

"That's what I'm asking you!" he groaned, instantly exasperated.

"I don't know. I can't remember."

There was no use pursuing it. It was part of the game now, a child's game in which a kid will withhold information or not answer correctly, for reasons that Marshall would never understand. But he knew there was a reason, that somewhere inside their conniving kids' minds they were waiting for something like love or pot brownies to let all their true feelings out. But too often, he realized, that chance never came and kids became fucked up adults, concealing emotions from lovers and friends and sometimes even themselves.

"It was 'Maniac'," said Esther. "Yeah, it was 'Maniac'," she confirmed, quashing all Marshall's beliefs about kids and the much older brats they become.

Marshall's most cherished memory of Beth Ann was pretty much captured in a photograph that sat alone on his bookshelf. He hadn't framed it or anything; it was just the print, already beginning to curl at the edges from moisture and exposure to sunlight. That's what Marshall thought about memories, that they shouldn't be protected or encased in a frame but allowed to linger and fade away with the natural passage of time. The photo itself was almost cheating, but he kept it anyway, right where he could see it, where he couldn't not see it from anywhere in his homemade little house.

The photo, taken by Beth with her tripod and flash, revealed the small table beside her bed, heaped with cut-glass dishes of cold cuts, cheeses, olives with toothpicks, wine goblets filled with pink milk. A heart shaped cake that Marshall had made himself—no small feat in his wood burning cookstove—was the centerpiece, surrounded by crystal dishes of red and white jellybeans, diced mangoes, strawberries with real whipped cream, and a bottle of ketchup, without which, for Beth Ann, no meal was truly complete. All of this lit by the light of red candles and equally bright red tulips. In the background of the photo, you can see the red and white streamers she'd draped around the room, drooped and gathered like campaign bunting above her bed, where the covers were drawn back invitingly. It was Valentine's Day, and the decorative bedroom and all that went with it were Beth Ann's gift to Marshall.

But first they had to play strip poker, the rules of which were surprisingly fluid and entirely dependent on Beth's discretion. Both players were allowed four articles of clothing, which for Marshall entailed a T-shirt, jeans, and both his socks. Beth's poker outfit consisted of a slinky tangerine colored dress, flimsy silk camisole, lacy antique bra and bikini underwear that tied in front with a little red bow. Marshall wouldn't have cared who won, but the fact that Beth cheated so ruthlessly turned the game into a hard-fought, hard-breathed battle wherein Marshall was finally forced to concede while Beth still retained her cute undies. By that time she was pretty much driving him crazy, sitting cross-legged across the bed, refusing his every entreaty.

"I'm bare-ass naked!" Marshall whined. "You whipped my boney butt!"

Smiling triumphantly, her one tooth leaning, Beth leaned forward to graze her lips on Marshall's hairy cheek. "Please be mine," she whispered softly, nuzzling close to his ear.

"Hell, yeah!" Marshall exclaimed, instantly groping, but Beth stayed his hand from her breast. Because next they needed a bubble bath, hot soapy water in the candlelit bathroom, steam floating up near the ceiling. Lying in the tub with Beth pressed against him, they kissed and squeezed, slipped and slid in a rainbowed frothing of bubbles, skin turning pink with replenished hot water when Beth turned the tap with her toes. They scrubbed with loofahs and scented bar soap, shampooed each other's hair, until so squeaky clean their skin felt transparent, buffed and polished like chrome.

Toweled off, half dry, their hair still wet, Beth led Marshall from the steamy bath back into her bedroom, goose pimples rising along her arm from the sudden chill in the air. Dashing toward the bed she pulled him down and they snuggled beneath the blankets, kneading, giggling, moving together in shapes they would never recall. And even then Marsh knew he was trapped, in love with a girl whose life was a series of elaborate, spontaneous rituals, from the moment she picked out a blouse in the morning to the novel she read that night, each choice was important, a momentous occasion requiring great celebration. He would always remember this Valentine's Day spent in the bubbly bathtub, in the welcoming arms of Beth Ann. How long she'd remember was anyone's guess, and anyone else would be right: not for too long, and likely not always deprived of a certain memento, an old, yellowed memory curling away on Marshall's dusty bookshelf.

"What's going on at the movies?" Marshall asked, knowing Esther would have conferred with her friends.

"I've seen almost everything," she sighed. "Tarzan twice. Footloose, too. Already seen Police Academy, but I guess I'd watch it again."

"Eh, no thanks. I doubt I could sit through that. We'll find something neither of us has seen."

Marsh marveled at kids' ability to absorb so many movies, any kind of movie, as long as there was action and a smattering of dialogue. Not too long ago Esther was into films like Friday the Thirteenth, Halloween, and any number of other blood and gore flicks. He couldn't watch even one, they freaked him out so. But today's kids laughed at that kind of stuff; it entertained the hell out of them. When would it start to bother them, he wondered, when would it all seem too real, the realization that bad shit happens in literal, blood dripping flesh?

Marshall despaired of his attempts to define maturity, and the older he got the vaguer the line between adolescence and adulthood became. Perhaps there was no threshold to cross. Marsh had been waiting for something like maturity to overtake him for some time, a sudden transformation akin to wisdom to wash over his life like a wave, leaving him cleansed, spiritually renewed, no longer a child playing soldier in the woods, hiding away in his fort.

He did have some dog-eared idea of maturity, a concept left over from Esther's age, a time full of cowboy movies, Little League struggles and Sunday School, and it was the direct result of those after-church lessons that he retained the age of thirty-three as the D-Day of maturity, the day when wisdom would storm the beaches and finally conquer confusion. Jesus was purportedly thirty-three years old when he died, and therefore that age acquired great meaning, representing a form of emotional climax akin to the feeling of orgasm. Well, Marshall was now thirty-three, and no one was attempting to nail him to a cross for the insight he'd accrued. In a way, logging was his crucifixion—hadn't he a bloody thumb to prove it? Except Marsh wouldn't die and rise again; his cross to bear was life itself, to live to log another day.

In truth, Marshall didn't feel especially persecuted, though he did enjoy dramatic thoughts about himself. And he'd never once compared himself to Jesus, though he did feel a certain affinity for the man, not necessarily on a personal basis—they both liked a beard—but on a planetary scale, humanity aspiring to Christ-like virtues, all shoulders pressed to the stone. And so, he felt it safe to say that in certain ways he was attempting to be like Jesus, minus the loaves and fishes. As they used to say, "the medium is the message," and currently Marshall's medium was love, spreading it around as best he could, at the risk of appearing too desperate.

"Whaddya think about Jesus, Ess?' he asked.

Surprised by the question, cocking her head, she shrugged a disinterested reply. "I dunno. He was alright I guess."

"Like fine, or just okay?"

"Jesus was cool, and kind of cute, if you believe those ancient paintings. Why, are you getting born again?"

"Hell no. Why go through all this twice?"

While there was a real difference between Marsh and Esther's age, he knew he'd never be able to put his thumb—mutilated as it was—on what that difference was. The only real evidence of how much they differed was that Esther could sit through ninety minutes of Texas Chainsaw Massacre without once closing her eyes.

Seeking to change the subject, he asked, "How's old Richie what's-his-name? You haven't mentioned him yet."

"Richie Vanderyacht."

"And how is Master Vanderyacht?"

"I dunno."

"How can you not know about the love of your life?"

He could see he'd touched a nerve, Esther's blonde head tilting back, the ends of her mouth drawn down. Marshall loved that look; it showed all her fine features, her narrow nose and almond-shaped eyes, much more beautiful and feminine than he felt an almost twelve-year-old required. She reminded him greatly of Faye in that moment, and he realized the look was more learned than genetic.

"I don't love Richie anymore," she informed him.

"Wow," said Marshall, truly surprised. "I thought you intended marriage?"

Too excited to feign offense, Esther blurted, "I love Carl Ballantine now! Carl Ballantine who's in sixth grade!"

"The Carl Ballantine? So recently of fifth grade and soon to be in seventh?"

Esther knew Marshall was poking fun but decided she didn't care. "He's the tallest boy in school, and he plays every sport, and got to go to the Young Writers Conference in Olympia!"

"Regular Rhodes Scholar. You've really traded up."

"Carl is not only smart, but his father is rich. He owns a big company and spends most of his time in Los Angeles and Boston."

"Sounds terrific. Maybe you'll live in New York, or Hoboken, or some other exotic locale. But what about ol' Richie Vanderyacht? How's he taking all this?"

"Fine, I guess. He's just the same. Plain old regular Richie."

"Hmm," said Marshall, tapping his thumb on the steering wheel.

"I mean, I still like him, but I love Carl Ballantine!" she said, and instantly punched up the volume of a song that just then came on the radio.

Once again it was time for Marshall to be amazed. How quickly things change in the fast-paced world of human emotion, how suddenly poor Richie had fallen into disfavor with a female member of the species. Are humans just much more resilient in their youth, that much more confident in life and themselves that crushing rejection does not affect them?

Marshall knew he was fooling himself. Kids at that age don't experience anywhere near the depth of emotional and psychological bonding that adult relationships entail. Yet he also knew that Esther felt she was truly in love with Carl Ballantine, who just might bite the bullet next week over some older, taller, more athletic future novelist whose father traveled to Hong Kong and Puerto Rico.

In the midst of her bouncing around to the music, Esther reached out and playfully snapped Marshall's suspenders, and in so doing noticed the letter stuffed in his shirt pocket. "Who's that from?" she asked.

"Carl Ballantine," he quipped.

"Is not! What's it really?"

"Suicide note from Richie V."

Knowing she was getting nowhere, Esther waxed philosophical. "You're silly sometimes, Marshall."

Marshall leaned and squeezed Esther's leg, sending her into a spasm of laughter. She seemed at that moment nearly hysterical with happiness, and he was struck by the little girl in her still, her face like that of a child on a swing, her penchant for joy living side by side with the waxing world of adult condescension and roll-your-own cigarettes.

"Hey!" Marsh shouted, cranking up the radio, gyrating around in his seat. "We're back in the video, groovin' the bed of the truck!"

Esther fell right into it, her high voice whooping, skinny arms flailing, blonde head bobbing like a dashboard doll. If Marsh was indeed silly, so be it, he thought; it kept him from feeling he was growing old, helped him survive another day. All around them at the four-way stop in Bellingham, fellow motorists craned their necks to observe the dancing duo in the bed of the pickup, a dented hard hat and one ghostly glove floating behind the wheel.

In the bottom of Beth Ann's Vaseline jar there's a nickel. Marshall noticed it one night when he and Beth were removing grease paint from their faces, balls of Kleenex confettied around them. It was late at night, or early morning, and they'd just returned from a wild, psychedelic Halloween party at the bar. Beth Ann had dressed as the female cybernaut from Blade Runner, her hair sprayed white and frizzed like a dandelion, upside down eyelashes grazing her cheeks like a couple of creepy spiders. A sleek satin leotard—midnight black—conformed to her body like a seal's skin.

Beth Ann, a theater student at heart, possessed an amazing assortment of makeup, including a collapsible, portable mirror with light bulbs that ran all around it. Earlier that evening Marshall had sat before the mirror for nearly an hour, playing with the tubes of greasepaint, making sure every line and contour he applied to his face was perfect. He had dressed as the Antichrist, with a blood red face, sinister black highlights, and a crown of thorns crafted from a strand of rusty barbed wire. Black pants, a borrowed motorcycle jacket, and rubber hip-waders completed the outfit, as well as a couple of sixteen-penny nails he'd fashioned with a hammer and vise that convincingly slipped between the fingers of each bloody hand.

Marsh won first prize at Graham's Halloween party, where he sat at the bar with monsters and fairies and half-naked people with bags over their heads, while Beth Ann, the manager/bartender, hissed around in cybernaut character serving drinks to well-disguised ghouls and goblins that rudely pinched her cute ass. Beth, who truly hated ass pinching, intimidated the hell of these assumingly male creatures, her costume the perfect manifestation of her feelings regarding the "public property" attitude that men held toward women.

When Graham's closed everyone headed up the hill to the Chandelier, a hard-liquor bar where another crowd of Halloween freaks had gathered, largely Canadian, one actually dressed as a cheesehead (won first prize) boogying down to a disco-oriented jukebox.

In keeping with the spirit of the evening, many of the locals present took to eating psilocybin mushrooms, and Marsh became quickly absorbed in the music, writhing in unison to the electronic drumbeats. Stripped to his t-shirt and stocking feet, he danced through pools of spilt beer and ice cubes to every song on the Wurlitzer, his hair soaking wet, beard encrusted with grease paint that melted like candle wax. Even between songs he couldn't sit still, rolling soggy cigarettes atop the beer-soaked bar, puffing them to life like a blacksmith's bellows before stumbling back to the dance floor. Meanwhile, unbeknownst to Marshall, Beth Ann—in her shiny black leotard—absorbed fresh abuse from a whole new supply of pinchers, some of whom she likely recognized. Marsh later thought that their behavior, combined with Beth's predisposition toward men, contributed greatly to the grief that was soon to follow.

"Why is there a nickel in your Vaseline jar?" he asked several hours later, his face and fingers slathered with petroleum jelly and cold cream. Both he and Beth looked totally creepy, like gelatinous larvae in pre-pubescence, creatures from the Black Lagoon.

"I can't remember. It was something, though. Like maybe my old friend Brenda . . ."

Marsh loved that kind of stuff about Beth, the secret things that held great meaning if only she could remember. He collected those things about her like other people collected stamps, or butterflies, colorful images on fluttering wings, there for a moment, then gone. One day last spring, driving past fields where horses grazed, Beth said, "Look at that grass! It's the same color green as those crayons I chewed as a kid!" That struck Marshall just right, and he conjured a picture of Beth in her bedroom, sampling Crayolas like Whitman's Chocolates, their labels peeled off all around her. Another night, lying in bed, she told him the story of a swimming pool party she'd attended in freshman year, her boyfriend a kid she'd known all her life, a longtime friend of the family. She'd found herself standing alone on the diving board with her classmates gathered around, singing a love song to Kyle or Ken or whoever the hell he was, "Cherish", "Venus" or "Precious Love"—she couldn't recall anymore. But Marshall remembered, and he could picture her still balanced out there on the board, even lankier then, undeveloped, and wearing a lime green swimsuit.

Pawing through his pockets with slimy fingers, he struggled to pull out a coin. "Here," he said, plopping it into the Vaseline jar, where it landed without a sound. "By the time you're old, you'll be flush with cash you can't remember anything about."

Nickels in jars, edible crayons, diving board serenades, these were the memories he wanted for his own, the odd recollections of Beth Ann's history like so many doors in a house, awaiting a key, or the pertinent question required for one to gain entrance.

She was wiping the last of the goop from her face, her afro collapsed on her shoulders, when Marshall said, "You're so beautiful, sweetie. Wish I had that camera now."

Beth's face shriveled in a vengeful glare and her blue eyes locked on his. "I'm so sick of hearing that kind of shit! Is that all guys can think of?" Throwing her Kleenex at the ticking wood-stove, she stormed off into the bathroom.

Steam from the shower drifted into the kitchen as Marsh sat dumbfounded on his stool. Plucking a butt from an overflowing ashtray, he lit it with Beth Ann's kleptoed lighter, the smoke and vapor swirling together like mist on a gothic moor. He stared at his hands, still painted red where they pinched the roach of the butt, his t-shirt stained with streaks of sweat from three solid hours of dancing. The barbed wire crown sat beside him on the counter, and sweeping it up he jammed it on his head in a gesture of monkish contrition, releasing a smoky, extended sigh that trembled away in a halo.

Marshall felt he was as capable as the next guy of recognizing the value in another human being, male or female, and did not believe that women were innately more adept at communicating with other women than men were. He'd spent so much of his life surrounded, engulfed, overwhelmed by females that it pissed him off to be told that his perception of one entire half of the species was somehow inferior, or incomplete, by virtue of the fact of his maleness. Can't a son know his mother, a brother his sister, a husband his wife or daughter?

It was hard not to feel resentful, and he was feeling that way now as he fingered another butt from the ashtray, the spiraling smoke only adding to an atmosphere of gloom and frustration. Marshall had been present at restaurants or campfires when Beth and some other woman exchanged views about politics, the feminist movement, how men were so fucking stupid. He guessed he should have felt flattered to be there, his maleness tolerated or perhaps just ignored while others of his kind got trashed. He must have been considered an "okay" man to be privy to such conversations, which as long as they were offered with humor and wit were not considered demeaning. Rather, they were part of an inside joke wherein it was cool, or even chic, to mimic male behavior, collecting nude magazines, comparing appendages—your standard meat-market mindset.

It had not been so casual, so convivial with Faye. Single mothers were perhaps the most desperate of their gender, always dreaming of independence but resigned to observe it from afar. How many times had he watched Faye's face as she cashed her meager paycheck or avoided the eyes of a grocery clerk as she paid for milk with food stamps? Men had hurt her—Marshall included, yet she hadn't held it against him, pressing herself against him instead, in an effort to make it all stop.

When the shower fell silent and the steam abated, he heard wet footsteps slap across the floor and turned to find Beth beside him, wet hair plastered in curls to her forehead, naked, and sparkling clean. With a towel in one hand and container of Johnson's baby powder in the other, she said, "I'm sorry, Marshall. I know you don't just want me for my body."

Which, of course, at that moment, he totally did, and grabbing the bottle of talcum powder he proceeded to pat down her shoulders, tattooing a pattern of red and white handprints across her still damp skin. Shrieking a giggle, she grabbed his hand and pulled him back to the bathroom, where enough steam arose to engulf the small house, condensing in drops on the windows.

Esther had no memory of her father. Not a face, a voice, or a fuzzy silhouette. In fact, her only memories of him were those few images provided by her mother of a tall, kind, goodhearted man who had loved her very much. Esther knew it wasn't true, that he'd abandoned Faye and their infant daughter and now lived somewhere in Alaska. And yet she went along with the story because her mother needed her to, and also because . . . why not? It was something to tell her friends when they asked, and sometimes even an obvious lie was better than nothing at all. The one true thing that could be said of her dad was that Faye always feared that John would return and try to take Esther away. And thus, there was always a mysterious man who lurked at the edge of their lives, threatening Esther and her diligent mom, who made sure every night that the door was locked and both the porch lights lit, who combed Esther's hair and tucked her in bed before heading downstairs to her room.

But Esther combed her own hair now, chose which clothes to wear, and Faye became the face that appeared in her doorway to tell Essie and her friends to turn down the volume, switch on a light, who crouched in the gravel fixing the chain on Esther's ancient ten-speed. Esther and her friends rode their bikes through puddles on bumpy old logging roads, across wooden bridges beneath canopies of trees where the sunlight barely shone through. Waiting at the bus stop they ignored the boys and danced to Sony Walkmans, spent the night at pajama parties in the homes of girls whose richer parents owned VCRs and Gameboys. Faye would be waiting in the car the next morning, sipping at a coffee from Graham's Store, waving through the windshield as the girls filed out the door. T-ball, soccer, she was always there, in a front row seat at the Christmas play, or standing on the porch with a spoon in her hand, shouting that dinner was ready.

Esther could feel herself getting older, sense it in the subtle differences, the emerging distances between herself and her mom. And she began noticing other things too: headlights sweeping through her curtained window, Earl's gruff voice at the door. She began to feel her mother's life as the separate thing it was, extending beyond her maternal role as Esther's sole provider, having needs of her own more important than cooking and purchasing Reebok sneakers. It scared her a little, and as a result she found herself hugging her mom at odd times, at the laundromat, in the checkout line, in a booth at a Mexican restaurant. And she began to feel that she didn't love her mother enough—not as much as Faye loved her, not nearly as much as Marshall loved Beth Ann.

Esther had wanted Marshall to be her dad, had confided to her mom that she wished she could call him Daddy. Faye had promised to ask him about it, but they never discussed it again. Esther could clearly remember them fighting, sometimes keeping their voices down, other times swearing out loud. Marshall swore a lot—he always did . . . "Who's gonna make the goddam payments? Whose gonna build the house? I am, that's who! So why are you giving me shit about dishes? You know I don't cook worth a fuck!"

They were going to buy land and build a house, which Marshall eventually did, cutting down trees, milling the logs, cutting the boards by hand. There was no electricity, but there was water in the creek and an outhouse back in the woods. It was totally Marshall's kind of place but not exactly Faye's. And definitely not Beth Ann's.

Esther could remember when Marshall had first moved in with her and her mom. He'd just returned from New York where something bad had happened, and he was quiet, sad, often sitting alone in his big old overstuffed chair, listening to records on a lopsided turntable he'd bucked off a console with his chainsaw. It made the music sound funny sometimes, propped up by bricks on one side. But Marshall didn't seem to care, and sometimes she'd wake up in the middle of the night to the sound of the music turned low and see Marshall's cigarette glowing in the dark, the shape of his head in the shadows.

They used to go hiking a lot back then, up to Keep Kool or Secret Lake, Winchester Lookout in the fall. Picnic lunches by waterfalls, wading in slow-moving pools, their legs turned white in the knee-lapping water, toes buried deep in the sand. Tiny fish darted through their forest of limbs and sometimes tickled their calves. "Piranha!" Marsh shouted, suddenly lunging to pinch at Esther's arm. Thanksgiving dinners, Easter egg hunts, trickertreat baskets of candy. . . they had seemed truly happy, like a real family should, pouring through pictures in photograph albums and tacking up birthday cards, searching for mushrooms in the cottonwood groves, making dandelion salads for potlucks.

One Christmas they all flew back to New York where Marsh and his sister Karen grew up, where his mom and niece still lived. The apartment building was made all of bricks and a whole city block in size, the biggest building that Esther had ever seen. New York was music and Christmas trees and colored lights strung between lamp posts, snowplows threading the narrow streets where cars were squashed up to the curbs. Esther and Kirsten played board games together on the big oval rug in the living room, a radiator hissing and soft lights blinking in Nonny's window display. A Christmas Carol was on TV one night, and Marshall explained that he and his sister had watched that movie on Christmas Eve for as long as he could remember. Esther closed her eyes for the spooky parts, but the movie was so old—in black and white—that lots of times they had to laugh at the antics of Tiny Tim. But Marshall mostly watched his mom, sneaking a peek over Faye's blonde head where it lay against his shoulder. Behind the glasses that hid her eyes, his mother appeared to be crying, snatching a Kleenex from the pocket of her robe, dabbing her cheeks on occasion. Marshall silently rose from the couch and reached for his pouch of tobacco, heading outside to smoke on the stoop until the movie was over, after Scrooge met the Spirit of Christmas Future and somehow became a changed man.

Women were mothers and men were fathers; that's how Esther saw it. At least until she was ten years old and Marshall and her mom broke up. Now he was something she couldn't define, hadn't the words to describe. A friend, an acquaintance, a used-to-be dad? Someone who'd once said he loved her? He liked her still, she was sure of that much; why else would they hang out together? But if Earl stuck around, would he be her dad? Who would Marsh be to her then?

There were always new people to fill in the blanks when someone important departed, like Marshall, like Earl, like maybe Beth Ann, and whoever came after that. Sleeping over on Beth Ann's couch she could hear them together at night, talking, laughing, reading aloud until finally the light blinked out. There were things that Esther would never understand until she became an adult. Only then would she learn how the world really worked, and why everyone left in the end.

R olling through the white striped parking lot at the mall, they passed a department store, bookstore, shoe store, stationery store, supermarket and twin movie theater. As well as a sporting goods store, music store, camera shop, smoke shop, and various fast-food franchises. If such places fascinated Marshall, they also repulsed him, squeezed in together with a feeling of compaction reserved for the walls of a canyon. But he loved to go to the mall with Esther, who was always so animated, so filled with excitement, that he felt as though he was tapping a current, plugged into her circuit of blinding white joy like a lightbulb screwed in a socket.

First they headed to the supermarket to pick out snacks for the movie, Esther prancing, leading the way in her immaculate, rainbow laced sneakers. Perusing the barrels in the bulk food section, Marshall felt self-conscious, dressed like a scarecrow in his dirty old work clothes, the elbows blown out of his hickory shirt and riggin' pants ripped to the knee. The clerks and stockers appeared to appraise him with something akin to suspicion, their sideways glances and narrowed eyes watching his every move, expecting he might sprint off any second with a gallon of Tokay wine. Yet he felt more at ease with Esther in tow, who dashed exuberantly from one barrel to the next, checking out carobs and Tootsie Roll pops, dried fruit shriveled like scrotums. What would an adorable girl like her be doing with a derelict bum? She wouldn't, of course, logic prevailing, so therefore he must be a logger.

His confidence restored, Marshall snapped plastic bags from their rollers with brazen, efficient aplomb, filling them with gourmet jellybeans and multicolored Mexican Hats. His mind distracted, he forgot to use the ladle attached to each barrel with a string, employing instead his grimy hand, which though gross and disgusting presented no problem until arriving at the health food section. Immersing his paw in a barrel of cashews, he whipped it back out in an instant, sending a fantail of salted nuts to rise in an arc toward the ceiling.

"Fuck! Shit! Dammit!" he swore, jamming his injured thumb in his mouth, licking the salted wound in his flesh until the pain began to subside.

"You really ought to wash that thing," said Esther, gliding up beside him. "At least put a band aid on it. You ready?"

Nodding, wincing, feeling a fool, Marshall shook his aching hand and childishly kicked the barrel. "Hardly hungry now," he mumbled. "That all you're getting?" he asked, observing the single bag in Esther's hand. "Fortune cookies, to take to a movie? How you gonna read them in the dark?"

Esther shrugged, averted her eyes, and Marshall only nodded. "Fine," he said, heading for the checkout, "a little sugar, some light reading. Gonna be a mystical night."

So they strolled through the mall guessing jellybean flavors: mocha, cinnamon, watermelon, peach, Esther reading her fortunes out loud, tossing the cookies in trash bins. "*The business of life is not measured in profit, nor leisure attained without work,*" she recited. "How stupid is that, Marshall? I don't even have a job!"

"*Sunset comes but once a day, but daybreak springs eternal.* Oh, come on," she complained, "this stuff is so corny. I thought they would tell us the future. Here, here's one for you."

"Nah, no thanks, I don't wanna know."

"C'mon, just one; I bought them for you!"

"For me?" he said, quickly acquiescing. "Okay, let's see what's in store."

Taking a cookie, he broke it in half, the pink slip of paper twirling away like a winged maple seed. His arm snapped out like a serpent's tongue and snagged the small ribbon midair—"You can never allow them to hit ground before you read the message. Otherwise," he warned, "the opposite will happen. I just made that up, but I'm pretty sure it's true."

Esther, a huge fan of making up rules, eagerly nodded her approval.

They were standing in a corridor of clothing stores—The Gap, Structure, Abercrombie and Fitch—where tall, skinny mannequins posed in the windows in varying degrees of undress, pretty young salesgirls not much older than Esther revamping the chic displays. Marsh at that moment felt equally naked, afraid in his soul to learn of the fate foretold by a dumb slip of paper. Pinching the fortune with his mutilated thumb, he summoned what courage he still possessed and recited his future aloud. *"Life is fleeting, passions wane, but love forever lingers."*

"That's great!" Esther squealed, rising on tiptoe, squeezing Marshall's arm. "It must mean Beth Ann! I love it! I love it! Let's do another, please?"

"Nah," he groaned, "One is enough. It's all just bullshit, you said so yourself."

Observing the look on Esther's face he decided to backtrack a little, adding, "Besides, as far as futures go, I'm better off sticking with this one," which deep within him he almost believed, now that he'd said it out loud.

Rolling the fortune in a tiny ball he flicked it over his shoulder, like tossing a penny in a wishing well or disposing of a burned-out roach. Back outside on the concourse sidewalk, the sky to the west had turned gold, the treetops aflame with the day's last hurrah before the sun fizzled out in the bay. Impatient as ever Esther walked backwards, coaxing Marsh to keep up, and tugged along like a dog on a leash he followed her aimless meander, traversing the sidewalk from end to end and window to plate-glass window, stopping to look at crowded displays of Nikon cameras, Adidas sneakers, and pyramids of bestselling books.

Circling one too many times, Marshall refused to continue. "Listen, Ess, I'm gonna collapse, pass out or something, if I don't smoke a cigarette. Why don't you hang here and check out the windows, I'll watch you from out in the truck."

"No way, Jose!" she forcefully objected, her face screwed up with the effort. "I don't want some creepy old guy yelling at me for no reason!"

Marsh knew in an instant he'd blown it again, and he chastised himself for forgetting. Yet more evidence of his sieve-like mind and lack of paternal instincts.

"Besides," said Esther, "I love how the smoke goes up your nose, how you make all those tiny rings. Who's gonna roll it, anyway? Me, that's who, so let's go."

The previous spring Marshall, Beth, and Esther had ventured into town for an evening of fun, food, maritime sunsets, and a much-needed respite from the sameness of small-town life. They started out at La Creperie, the only French restaurant in Bellingham, where they ordered shrimp, spinach, and strawberry crepes with dark roasted coffee and curiously tall, thin goblets of red wine. Esther had milk tinted pink with liqueur that she sipped with her pinkie extended, pretending an air of sophistication she'd gleaned from old black and white movies.

Marshall and Beth held hands the whole time, leaning across the tiny table to lavish each other with kisses. Their frequent displays of public affection were famous in the small town of Glacier, tolerated, ignored, or sometimes mocked by those without love of their own. Esther engaged in the affection as well, hugging, cuddling, her blue eyes smiling, skinny arms wrapped around shoulders. Beyond the tall windows the bay appeared stippled with diamonds of afternoon light, billowing sails as white as the clouds in a pastel foretelling of sunset.

The high-ceilinged room was pretty much empty, a lone guitarist sitting not far away with his feet on the rungs of a stool, plucking the notes of familiar old songs as delicate and fine as French crepes. Drawn into the mood of the happy trio he engaged them in light conversation, and when the crepes and wine and coffee were gone he dedicated a song to Marshall and Beth that he professed to have written himself, a love song, of course, both angsty and joyous, much like the couple themselves. And when the last note faded from the sunlit room the few other diners applauded, and Marshall believed they were clapping for them, for Esther, Beth Ann, and him, for the obvious love that glowed from within like the candle that lit their small table.

After dinner they cruised down State Street in Beth Ann's green-and-white Bug, the girls singing show tunes that Beth knew by heart, Esther shooting her squirt gun through opened windows at stop signs and passing cars. They spotted a friend's van parked at a tavern and Beth talked Marshall into stopping, hoping to entice their friend away for an evening of sunset watching at Boulevard Park.

Standing on the sidewalk in front of the bar, Marshall gave Esther instructions. "Wait right here where I can see you. Ten minutes tops, I promise."

Crowded around a table with Jim and Mayak and several of their friends, Marshall and Beth sat squashed in a chair with Beth on Marshall's lap, the tavern door open not ten feet away where Esther swung on a parking meter, shooting water straight up in the air and attempting to catch it in her mouth.

Someone of course bought a pitcher of beer, of which all were obliged to partake. "Just one, and we'll share it," Marshall told Beth, his one eye peeled toward the door. So they sipped and chatted and watched the clock, waiting for dusk to arrive, occasionally pelted with streams of water that Esther sharp-shot from the sidewalk. Near the end of their beer, and Marshall's patience, they realized they hadn't been soaked for a while and Beth stepped outside to see why. Esther sat huddled against the wall with her forehead pressed to the bricks, crying in shuddering, silent sobs, the squirt gun smashed on the sidewalk.

"What the hell happened?" Marshall demanded, suddenly kneeling beside her. He turned Esther's chin to see her face but she tugged her head away.

"A man!" she cried, "a stupid drunk man who tried to take my pistol. He said this was a fag bar, and I was a fag, and he just kept yelling and swearing!"

Marshall rose with his hands clenched in fists and glared both ways up the block, searching for the asshole, the cocksucking prick, the bag-licking, stump-fucking, ignorant cull who had ruined their perfect spring evening. A man, she had said, a stupid man who just kept swearing and yelling!

Marshall was so tired of defending men that he'd pretty much given up trying. Why couldn't a woman be the villain for once? Why was it always a male? There were plenty of asshole women around—Imelda Marcos, Eva Braun, AnitafuckingBryant. He wished Margaret Thatcher would stroll up the street so he could punch her right in the chomps! But then he'd get arrested and jailed for assault, and he and his penis would catch holy hell from Beth and her ball-busting friends. There was no way out, and no way back to the person he'd been before, before Beth Ann and the things she believed about women and, conversely, men. "It takes two to tango," he'd always heard said, a wives' tale made up by a husband.

Foregoing the sunset, the ride home was silent, Esther curled up in the narrow back seat, Beth Ann staring out the window. Marshall had offered to buy a new squirt gun, but his offer had been declined. He tried to remember the words to the song the guitarist had sung at the restaurant, stuff about sharing, hope, and love, the usual three chord drivel. But the tune itself had stuck in his mind and he hummed it under his breath, alone at the end of his own private diving board, a dark canyon yawning beneath him.

Sitting on the opened tailgate of the truck, Esther produced a passable cigarette, an angular, saliva-stained, cylindrical totem with tobacco protruding from both ends.

"Whoa," said Marshall when she reached toward his pocket where the letter from Beth protruded.

"Matches?" said Esther. "I was just gonna light it for you."

"No, you're not. You're not doing any such thing," he chastised. "Smoking is a terrible, dangerous habit. I shouldn't even be doing it around you, much less letting you roll them."

"Mom says they kill you."

"And she'd be right."

"So why? Why do you do it?"

The gazillion dollar question, Marshall thought, feeling guilty again, his default emotion of late. "It's hard to explain, Ess. It's one of those stupid, adult-type things we figure most kids can't handle."

"Like addiction," she said, serious as. . . cancer.

Sighing inside, Marshall stared at the various storefronts replete with their corporate logos, willing the jumble of mismatched letters to spell out some means of instruction: Deflect; Dissemble; Condescend flashing in neon lights. Addiction was difficult to understand even when you were in it. Especially then, he had to admit, having witnessed its grip from all angles.

"It's like sugar," he said, observing Esther nibble at a fortune cookie. "Sugar is one of the worst things you can do to your body, and yet here we are popping jellybeans, gobbling cookies, filling our bellies with garbage. Shit, I'm hungry," he suddenly realized, "we need to score us some chow. Whaddya say, kiddo? Tacos, Chinese, a Godfather's salad?"

"Nah," said Esther, half the bag of cookies depleted, her fate confettied across the blacktop, literally tossed to the wind.

"Let's catch a movie then, grab something to eat later. I'll even see Police Academy if you want."

"I don't need to see it again. I don't really feel like the movies."

Suddenly sullen, Esther corkscrewed a strip of pink paper around her slender finger, her long legs swinging off the lip of the tailgate, nearly touching the ground. When Marshall snatched the fortune from her hand she didn't even look up. It read: *When past becomes present the future retreats. Expectations may change.*

Marsh took to twisting the fortune around his own finger, bending it back upon itself in a half-ass Möbius strip. He knew exactly what Esther was thinking, had lived with the same thought for years. Faye's fear of her husband and his possible return had long been a touchy subject, Marshall dismissing her legitimate concerns with a casual wave of his hand. "He's not coming back, so stop talking about him. You're making the poor kid paranoid."

But Marshall had other reasons for wanting the subject dropped. Faye, in fact, rarely spoke about John in Esther's presence, answering her daughter's questions about him in the cheeriest and vaguest of terms. Marshall and Faye had held serious discussions about Esther's future, what would happen to her if something bad occurred. "If anything happens to me," Faye had said, "I want you to raise Essie. I don't want John in her life."

Marshall knew Faye's concerns about her daughter were genuine, but he also knew she wanted that same security for herself, that she still harbored dreams of love and a family that had led her to marry at the age of eighteen.

But Marshall didn't share that dream, and never had. He'd always been a drifter, a floater, pursuing the independent lifestyle, and Faye's subtle pressure brought him to wonder what exactly he was doing in such a relationship, why he was sharing a house, a life, a patently lopsided dream. He had fallen into their lives like someone falling from a great height, from a mountain or a ladder or a tall brick building, wanting something or someone to break his fall before he struck rock bottom. And Faye had been waiting with open arms, as women often were, themselves in a freefall through what felt like love but was really the thinnest of air.

Truth was, Marshall hadn't much liked himself in his time with Faye and Esther, hiding all those parts of his life that he'd just as soon forget. And in his reluctance to make a lasting commitment he was being honest with himself, but with no one else, his hesitancy reflected in everything he did and most of the things he thought, eventually not sharing any of his thoughts until Faye finally left him—for another man, another dream, another last chance at love.

But it wasn't all his fault, he'd told himself. Faye had her own demons, her own self-doubt, emotional needs beyond the means of one man to supply. She'd put all her eggs in Marshall's frayed basket, ignoring the hole in its bottom.

Plucking the chaff from Esther's cigarette, he paused before striking a match, then stuffed it in the pocket of his riggin' shirt where all his postponements were filed. "Okay," he said, "I know exactly what you need. C'mon, you wanna drive?"

"Yeah!" enthused Esther, instantly rejuvenated.

"Whoa now, girl! I was only kidding."

Just as quickly deflated again, Esther lowered her chin to her chest and resumed her sulking fugue state.

It truly killed Marshall to see her this way, the way he had so often seen her, especially those times when he was to blame. "Okay, okay," he heard himself say, observing his movements as if from above as he strode around the truck to the driver's side and opened its creaking door. "Madame," he said, proffering a hand as Esther leaped into the cab. Racing quickly to the other side, sliding down in the seat, "Wait a second!" he shouted too loudly when Esther reached for the key. "Don't you wanna know how it works?"

"I already know. I've watched you forever. You jiggle the stick and go."

"Kind of," said Marsh, "you're almost right. But there are a few moves in between."

He briefly availed her of which pedal did what and what to expect when she pushed it, thinking, Faye will kill me if she ever finds out. If Esther and I survive. Committed now, he called upon that reserve of calm that all thirty-three-year-olds possessed, fishing for serenity as if on a pond, casting his line on its placid surface devoid of all ripples and rings. He was still trolling when Esther reached and turned the key. In lieu of a functioning parking brake the tranny had been left in first gear, and without the advantage of engaging the clutch, the truck lurched forward and instantly died. When Esther looked up her eyes were wide and her mouth conformed to an oval, her braces revealed like the grill of a car, a classic '58 Buick.

"That's alright," Marshall soothed, wary of causing a meltdown. "Ease off on the clutch as you step on the gas. But slowly, slowly, like stirring a pot, or petting a dog you just met."

Esther did as instructed, and before they knew it they were rolling over the painted white lines of the mostly empty parking lot, oblivious to the rules those lines implied, content—no, enchanted—to be moving forward in a more or less straight line. Esther sat rigid with her hands on the wheel in the ten and two position, her tongue protruding to lick at her lips as though lapping an ice cream cone. Upon attaining the speed of ten miles per hour, Marshall leaned toward her with his hand on the dash and said, "Okay, Essie, shift!"

The first time she tried, the gears ground cruelly, Marshall grinding some teeth of his own while maintaining an encouraging smile. But the second attempt went smoothly enough that he felt his heartbeat subside, its rhythm decreasing in direct proportion to the engine's rpms. At that same moment, from the corner of his eye, he observed a blue van with Canadian plates enter the mall's main entrance, pursuing a trajectory aligned with their own that portended near certain collision. Esther appeared unaware of its presence and the potential for imminent impact, while inside the van a family of Pakistani Canadians, replete in a palette of colorful turbans, stared in horror—or at least great suspense—at the small white pickup's approach. Marshall was about to grab the wheel when Esther, with unpracticed precision, depressed the clutch and turned the wheel in one simultaneous motion, gliding the truck in a wide, smooth arc before braking in front of the Cineplex.

Turning toward Marshall with a euphoric grin, Esther's eyes sparkled with the vibrant colors of the neon theater marquee, her own inner glow shining through its veneer like a lighthouse slicing through fog. Marshall really wanted that cigarette now, but instead he reached for a fortune cookie and popped it whole in his mouth, halting mid-chew to fish out the paper stuck to the tip of his tongue. Holding it up in the fading light he pretended to read its inscription, "The paths of life shall intersect; mysterious strangers soil their pants."

Divining the need for a speedy escape, the duo switched places and Marshall piloted them quickly and cautiously across town, pretending great stealth in checking the rearview as if they were being pursued. By the time they pulled up to the curb at Pet Village, it was dark, the lights through the windows falling in yellow rectangles across the parking lot, painting the shadows of parrots and monkeys to animate the rolling sidewalk.

A small silver bell announced their entrance, and the

redolent perfume of dampness and dung quickly overwhelmed them, lending the place a tropical feel in the presence of so many lives. Tall, spreading palm trees and potted plants grew between various cages, where dozens of colorful, squawking birds strutted and bobbed their heads, pink and gray love birds, green and blue parakeets, minas with long curving beaks. Hunched like old men on their wooden dowel perches, parrots rocked slowly with half-hooded eyes that gazed deep into Marshall's own, sometimes hooking their beaks on the cage to hang their full weight from the bars. Farther down the aisle a fake-looking waterfall gurgled over blue-painted lumps, eventuating in a shallow, kidney-shaped pool where turtles, newts, and salamanders languished on its dun-colored shore. Snakes of all stripes—literally and figuratively—slithered around on plastic sand the colors of the national flag, their scaly skin gleaming, forked tongues darting at the walls of their glass enclosure.

Esther let go of Marshall's hand and floated away on her own, leaving Marshall to gape with ill-concealed awe at the wonder of life all around him. A cylindrical cage filled with hundreds of songbirds rose from floor to ceiling, their chirping, trilling chorus of voices woven in an intricate, natural harmony born of collective genetics. Flashing wings formed a spectrum of color from red to orange to blue, huddled together in conga line fashion to sing their songs and bump their beaks in an avian version of kissing.

Farther along were the rodent cages: gerbils, hamsters, and neurotic white mice, some spinning wildly on metal wheels while others lay burrowed in the sawdust. One tiny critter with weird red eyes nursed four even tinier babies, bald as a pinkie and half as big, blind to the huge world around them. Black and white rats rose on hind legs to curiously sniff at the air, their paws held before them as though begging for alms or clutching a miniature hat.

Faye and Esther had always kept rats. One, Vanessa, had survived for nearly two years, surprising them all with her bug-eyed vitality. Marshall still had Vanessa's cage—a repurposed fish tank—stored beneath his bed where it gathered dust and spiders and misplaced books. One time, back in the rodent days, they'd all been driving home from town when a squirrel ran out in front of the truck and beneath the right front tire. Two big rules of life with Faye were that you always buried a dead critter when you found one, and never, ever, hit one on the road without stopping to see if it was hurt. That time the squirrel was still alive, unconscious but whole and unbloodied. Faye and Esther wrapped it in a sweater and took it straight home to Glacier, where they fed it milk and seeds and love until the second day, when lo and behold, it appeared quite hale and hardy. The third day found it stiff as a board, stone dead in the sawdust of Vanessa's old aquarium.

Marshall preferred dogs, big furry creatures strong enough to hug and wrestle around with. Esther had grown up with three or four litters of puppies, almost one per year in the time they'd lived together. Puppies were the most literal expressions of love and new life imaginable, so trusting and happy and excited for more, more, more! He remembered when he was Esther's age and had wanted a puppy so badly, an untenable prospect while living in an apartment, courting the ire of one's neighbors. But when his father died, he finally got one, a female of course, portending the ratio of men to women for the rest of his outnumbered life. His mom had taken him to the sad little pet shop in the basement of Masters Department Store, hidden amidst mattresses, rolls of carpet, and boxes of linoleum tiles. Shoved in a corner of cinderblock wall, a dozen little hearts beat wildly, licking at fingers that poked through their cages, tails slapping the newspaper floor. Watching the salesman pluck a puppy from its cage, Marsh held out his arms in reserved expectation as the pup whined and wiggled midair, its bluish eyes wide in attempting to focus, its pink belly smooth as a peach. Feeling its warmth against his chest when finally it lay in his arms, something inside him burst like a dam, bringing literal tears to his eyes, an outpouring of love for the milk-breath creature snuggled beneath his chin. Puppies loved everything and anything they encountered in their stumbling embrace of the world, greeting each day with the same blind hope as they had the day before, and in Marshall's own struggle with passage and loss he believed that the pup had saved him, revealing how life was renewed in each moment, with each eager lick of its tongue.

Marsh realized now what a true act of love and compassion his mother's gesture had been, and he pictured her standing alone between cages, clutching her purse to her chest, the very same tears in her own blue eyes, not a month since the death of her husband. What had she been thinking as she watched her young son—her own pup of sorts—as he cuddled that baby to his cheek? Was she thinking of her children, of Marshall and Karen, and how they might reckon with death? Or was she thinking of Al, her partner in life, and what he might make of this moment, her desperate attempt at providing salvation in the midst of so much grief. She certainly hadn't been thinking of herself, as she never had once in her life, as she wouldn't in the future through the hard years to come when love could provide no solution.

And here were those same puppy faces now, innocent, adorable, unabashedly joyous as they tumbled and growled in comic parody of the larger dogs they would soon become. One little white one gnawed aggressively at Marshall's hand, yipping, growling, pouncing theatrically as Marshall egged him on. He wanted so badly to get some small creature for Esther; not a dog, of course, that would have to be Faye's decision, but some baby animal with blood and a heart and an all-consuming need. He spotted Esther in a darkened back room bent toward the glow of a fish tank, her blonde hair hanging in a curtain to her knees, nearly obscuring her face. Her expression was so serious, so somber and stern that he squinted to make sure it was her and not some older pink-sweatered girl in identical, rainbow laced sneakers.

Entranced by the bubbly, glowing little world in which the equally glowing little fish existed, Esther followed their circuit along the glass in endless, repetitive circles, some so tiny and lacking in substance their skeletons shone through their transparent skin whenever they passed by the light, others so sleek and hi-tech in design they might have been sketched by a draftsman. Yellow and blue, round and flat, polka-dotted and striped, their gills filled like bellows and their black eyes blinked, side fins flashing to keep them upright like coins spinning round on a table. They swam though an aerated, watery world of ghostly purple light, arrays of pink coral rising like trees amidst hula-skirt patches of seaweed. Ceramic castles and shipwrecked boats leaned sideways in the plastic sand, seashells dotting the lumpy bottom to mimic the floor of an ocean.

The tragic thing about pet store creatures is they all look so desperate to escape. How does a fish look desperate? Esther thought. Perhaps in the way their big lips pouted and their soft noses pressed to the glass, how their tail fins flapped in staccato bursts as though willing the water to part. She'd stood before every tank in the room and none of the fish looked happy, confused by all the castles they could not enter and the ships that had never once sailed. Did they somehow sense that beyond the glass was a world that forbade their survival, where they'd all die gasping by her sneakered feet on the cold linoleum floor?

Pressing her forehead to the side of the tank, she fluttered her big blue eyes. The fish didn't seem to notice at first, or at least they didn't let on, so she fell to humming a mindless tune in hopes they could feel the vibration, to breech in that fashion the aquatic divide and share her thoughts with fish. The cold of the glass where her skin pressed against it was beginning to give her a headache when suddenly Marshall's distorted mug appeared on the other side.

"Kiss a fish, five cents," he said, making a smooching sound, his lips pressed flat to the slimy glass like banana slugs climbing a window.

"Really gross, Marshall!" Esther protested. "Don't ever try

to kiss me again!"

"Hey, these lips are quite popular in some circles."

"If Beth Ann could see you now, she'd never let you kiss her again."

The silly comment hurt Marshall somehow, and for a second he couldn't reply. "Then please don't tell her," was all he came up with, quickly adding, "but hey, seriously, how 'bout we get us a fish or something, like maybe one of these turtles? I still have that fish tank under my bed, and we could—"

But Esther was already drifting away, pausing beneath the fluorescent lights to allow her sight to return. Her eyes, when she turned to him, were glossy and pink, and she sniffled, sighed, and tossed her long hair before moving off down the aisle. "Hi, little pups!" he heard her say when she reached the canine section, crouching, duckwalking from cage to cage as the puppies all whimpered and whined.

How he wished Beth Ann could be with them now, tickling, cooing, inciting the puppies to even more joyful dog-ness. She'd know what to do at a moment like this when Marshall felt lost at sea, sunk to the bottom of his personal fish tank, strewn with the hulks of ghost ships. Beth could take the tiniest ember of joy and wave it like a sparkler overhead, scrawling words, drawing pictures to hang in the air for what felt like whole minutes at a time. He realized then just how much he'd miss her and how much his life would be changed, not having her there to temper his moods, to direct his attention to the moment, not the past or the future but the bright shining present that sparkled their names in the sky.

As if in response to Marshall's thoughts, Esther rose and glanced his way before striding off farther down the aisle, leaving the puppies tumbled on their backs, soulfully mourning her departure. Unable to bear their plaintive cries, Marsh felt compelled to replace her and knelt on the floor with both hands on the cage as the puppies returned to their licking, keeping one eye on their wiggling antics and the other trained on Esther.

There was only one monkey, one of those long-tailed, emaciated kind that looked as though it were wearing a Lone Ranger mask. Hunched forlornly in a corner of its cage, it peered through the glaze of the steamed-up window at colored blobs moving in the night, headlights, taillights, red and green stop lights diffused by the slick condensation. Little more than an infant, maybe two months old, it responded to none of Esther's attempts to attract its unfocused attention, not the placating tone of her soothing voice or her pale finger poking through the bars. "Hey little monkey," he heard her say as she rose on the toes of her sneakers, but the poor creature sulked with its narrow back turned and its tail tucked tight to its haunches, its sad little face reflected in the glass where its warm breath beaded the pane.

Observing Esther's failed attempts to communicate with the monkey, a primate species so similar to his own, Marshall recalled how some animals—tigers, eagles, elephants, giraffes—mate for life, never taking another lover if their chosen soul mate dies, much like his mom after her husband died, similar to the way his sister despaired of sharing a love that would last.

Tall and thin with long blonde hair, Karen had looked much like Esther, the same wan smile and drifting eyes that hinted at introspection, easily devolving into tight-lipped frowns and brooding, sulking dismissal. As kids, at night on the upper bunkbed, Marshall told jokes to his older sister, dumb, made-up stories that weren't even funny but that never-the-less made her laugh. Kittens in boxes, driving for ice cream, apple walks with their parents, she continued to laugh until she couldn't anymore, and Marsh couldn't figure out why. Was it something he said, or someone he was, or someone his sister became? Could Marshall have helped her way back then when Karen was Esther's age, if he'd know what to look for, what despair even looked like, if he hadn't himself been despairing? Do little girls in platinum curls really grow up to lose all hope and hurl themselves from rooftops?

The silver bell tinkled as Esther exited the pet shop, pausing briefly on the sidewalk to assess the situation, calculating the height of the window from top to bottom, to where the outline of the monkey appeared on the glass. A round wooden planter stood by the door, a sad little tree struggling to grow from its cigarette butt-stippled soil. Attempting to move it in line with the cage, she shoved and rocked and finally kicked it into place, panting from the effort, yet satisfied with the results. Stepping up on the planter's rim, she balanced with one hand gripping the tree and the other poised on the window. Raising that hand, she closed it in a fist and rubbed a small oval on the glass.

Marshall could only stare at the hunched shape of the monkey, his own body crouched in similar fashion while the yipping, growling, tenacious puppies jousted and licked at his hand. In the midst of his mindless perambulations, a needle-like tooth broke the scab of his thumb and found its way down to the bone. With his mouth opened wide in a silent scream, he never stopped watching the monkey, and just then an oval appeared on the glass and Esther's blue eyes were revealed.

Balanced precariously on the wobbly planter, Esther stared raptly at the monkey's face just inches from her own. It was a beautiful little face, stoic, expressionless, yet somehow filled with emotion. Whispering hoarsely, as if to herself, she said, "Hi, baby. Hi, monkey." Then again, a bit louder, repeating the heartfelt greeting. But her words only served to fog the glass and she wiped it again with her hand. The monkey, appearing to stir from its torpor, turned its dark head toward the movement, prompting Esther to tap on the glass with the tip of a nail-bitten finger. The monkey's round eyes, in attempting to focus, blinked in welcome surprise, and opening its mouth as if to speak, it pressed its small hand to the glass. And what a miraculous hand it was! Never had she seen anything so miniature, so perfect, the tiny fingers so much like her own, the cross-hatch of intricate lines on its palm like the myriad veins of a leaf! Pressing her fingertip flat on the glass she touched the monkey's hand, if only metaphorically, and if only in her mind, where all best intentions reside. "Hi, baby!"

she giggled, bursting inside. "Someone will love you soon!"

Marshall could tell that Esther was smiling, the clear glass oval framing her eyes like a sequined party mask. A clenched fist of tension relaxed inside him, and holding his bloody hand to his chest, he rose and headed for the door. But he didn't open it, and instead stood waiting until Esther's finger vanished from the window and the silver bell tinkled overhead. Triumphant and smiling, Esther was exuberant as the heavy door closed behind her, and she reached for Marshall's one good hand and gave it a mighty squeeze.

"I can't buy you that monkey," he blurted.

"I know. I know you would if you could."

Releasing a genuine sigh of relief, he squeezed her cold hand in return. "But please, Ess, let's get something, huh? Some warm little creature—"

"Okay!" she piped, her happiness returned. "You look like you could use a smoke," she added, conferring a kindness of her own, then danced down the aisle with her blonde head bobbing, fingers snapping—"Doo-doo, dot-dot. Thrillaaaah! In! The! Night!"

Reaching through the opened window of the truck, Marshall grabbed his tobacco from the dash and rolled a quick one, leaning on the fender, watching Esther through the pet store window as she walked, kneeled, crawled between cages. Fumbling through his pockets for a match, his hand came to rest on Beth Ann's letter, and he yanked it away as though scorched. Fuck, he admonished, quit whipping yourself, stash it in the glove box or under the seat until you're ready to read it. Or don't read it, rip it up, throw it away, be done with it once and for all! But nah, he conceded, that wasn't his style; he'd leave it in his pocket as a constant reminder, a proverbial thorn in his side, much like his thumb that hurt like hell just rolling a damn cigarette. He could have just wrapped the finger in duct tape and avoided all the pain, but an ounce of prevention was far too heavy compared to ignoring the cure, so instead he'd rubbed literal salt in his wounds and then stuck his hand in a fan blade. In keeping with long-held family tradition when dealing with things of this nature, it was better to wear your heart on your sleeve than squirrel it away in some ribcage.

Lighting the match in the cup of his hands, his fingers were limned in orange, and within the dark creases and slow healing wounds he envisioned the path of his life, calloused, scabby, fluted like bark from years of hard work in the mountains, a quiet life nurtured while cursing the silence, solitude wasted alone, not shared with another in candlelit rooms with the patter of rain on the roof. Leaning back on the hood of the truck, he blew out a long plume of smoke, watching it vanish in tremulous rings against the dark blue of the night.

The thing about Beth Ann that Marshall would miss the most was that she was always talking, and the fact that she did so required that he talk back. Because Beth insisted on some form of response, even if just a hmm or a huh, there had to be recognition, audible proof of the moment shared, of something transpired between them. And so it was in this awkward fashion that Marshall learned to talk, to speak of mundane, insignificant things that had once seemed unimportant, and to relate so many of them, and so unselfconsciously, that they took on great significance, revealing those parts of himself and his life that had previously felt like a secret.

Beth's only secret was that she had none, that there was

nothing about herself that she wouldn't or couldn't reveal. It didn't take long to figure that out, so it wasn't a secret for a long, and that's why she could talk about books or Greek food with the same intensity that she spoke about her father's alcoholism. Marshall had heard all about Beth's dad; he could picture his face, smell his harsh breath, hear his angry, gravelly voice as he swore and swung out at Beth's mom. But so, too, could Marshall taste the tiropitas, savor the lime-green crayons. He felt Beth's life like the wound that it was and was touched that she wanted to share it, and to share it with him of all people, the keeper of secrets, concealer of feelings, the much darker half of their moon.

Because they loved to watch the moon together. He remembered a night in August when they lay on their sleeping bags in the Yellow Aster Meadows, tanned and naked as the full moon cast their bodies a cool, burnished bronze. They'd spent the day swimming in the high mountain lakes, talking and napping and making love. And they were still talking when the moon rose, bathed in its light, lying in each other's arms. Beth told Marshall of the myriad things she wanted to do, the kinds of people she wanted to be. She was excited, ecstatic, sometimes confused. For her, watching the moon meant tracking its path, recording its journey across the sky from dusk to breaking dawn. But to Marshall the moon was a static orb, a lantern suspended in air. The fact that it traveled was inconsequential, a poetic conceit of the gods. The moon never moved so fast or so far that its mountains and craters were blurred, that its cusp of shadow lost its edge in distinguishing dark from light.

He remembered telling Beth that if he couldn't describe where his life was headed he at least understood where he'd been, fitting the parts and pieces together like some kind of jigsaw puzzle, each moment and memory separate yet whole, bright dots in a pointillist painting. Sweeping an arm across the chrome landscape, a grand and magnanimous gesture, he'd explained that this was all he wanted, that peace and beauty were all he required, what he hoped to receive from life.

Beth had remarked how different they were, kissing his cheeks, his neck and forehead as she spoke of it. Their multitude of differences had been apparent from the start, not the least of which their age. But there had been no real secrets, there could be no surprises. For them, in those days, that was inconsequential, the product of gross overthinking. Watching the moon and picking wildflowers was all they hoped to accomplish, their day-to-day feelings and eye-to-eye moments eclipsing all concepts of time, a waxing and waning of fiery passion that rushed in and out like a tide.

One rainy morning as they lay in Beth's bed, not long after Valentine's Day, a gray light fell through the one high window, revealing the tops of bare trees. Marshall was yawning, still half asleep when Beth leaned across him and snatched her journal from the now famous, much photographed table. Naked, cross-legged, curls framing her face, she read aloud from an ancient entry she'd written about her childhood. Marshall lay staring at the bare black branches as the words poured out of Beth Ann, scenes of her father beating her mother, Beth and her brother huddled together to weather the recurring storm. An image of a knife, an angry threat, a young girl's struggle with adolescent rage and the desire to hurt her father: these were the pictures Beth painted with her words, each framed by a pane of the window.

Absorbed in the scenes playing out in his head, it was difficult for Marshall to incorporate their image with his many other pictures of Beth Ann, alone on the diving board, dancing at the prom, her first awkward kiss in the back of a car before throwing up out the window. He'd seen the real photos, snapshots of Beth on a raft at the beach, on roller skates in Spokane, she and her brother in bulky snowsuits creating the shape of a snowman. There were not enough panes in the window to contain them all, and after a while he quit trying, lying under blankets with tears in his eyes and an odd sense of hope in his heart, thinking this was the closeness, the depth of emotion that people should take from each other, and although it hurt him to feel Beth's pain, it was also wonderful to share it. The sharing of grief was an animal thing, as dogs lick the blood from another dog's wounds, as moms kiss the bruised knees of their children.

The sharing of Beth's grief made her seem marvelous to Marshall, and the fact that she offered it so easily and honestly made him feel guilty that he hadn't, or couldn't, that he was likely incapable of ever returning the favor. And then as if by some kind of miracle, the miracle being Beth Ann, he heard his own voice in the dimly lit room as she snuggled her body against him, squeezing his arm, coaxing him on with the butterfly kiss of her eyelashes.

He told her about his father's car wreck that had left him partially paralyzed in the last year of his life, describing himself at twelve years old as he and his sister took turns strapping the metal brace on Daddy's leg, carrying a dinner plate down to the corner drugstore where their father wiled away the hours in the company of other men. Telling the story, exhuming the details, he noticed Beth Ann staring up at the window, through it and beyond it to a place filled only with her imaginings.

"The Christmas that Faye and Esther came with me to New York we visited my Aunt Edith's house on Elizabeth Street. I hadn't been there in many years, and seeing it again brought back memories of holidays and birthday parties, a mortgage-burning barbeque where Aunt Signe marched around the yard pretending to play the bagpipes, one hand pinching the bridge of her nose, the other cupped under her arm pit. "Wah! Wah!" she pretended to play as we kids trailed behind her like a kite's tail.

"Faye sat by my side at the kitchen table where we all sipped glasses of wine, Aunt Mildred, Aunt Gloria, and Cousin Peg, a gray-haired cabal of older women wherein I was the only man. Aunt Ruth told a story about Uncle Billy, about one of his practical jokes, and we all laughed hysterically, tipsy on memories as well as pink Chablis. When her turn came around, my mom told a story about my dad and her in the long months after the car wreck, how the two of them struggled to make awkward love, and how Al tumbled out of the bed. Everyone hooted and laughed but me, paralyzed by the knowledge, the realization that my parents had been just like me, struggling to learn how to love one another in what little time they had left.

"The red checkered tablecloth, Faye's face in profile, my mom sitting rigid in a straight-backed chair with her wedding band still on her finger . . . that is a picture I'll keep forever, a memory of a memory from my parent's past as seen through the lens of a wine glass."

His cigarette burned down to the roach, Marshall exhaled a last plume of smoke and glanced toward the window of the Pet Shop, where he could see Esther, just her shape through the glass, remonstrating angrily at the woman behind the counter.

"Fuck me," he swore beneath his breath, "asleep at the wheel again." Tossing the butt, he lunged toward the door where the jingling bell announced his return.

Seeing him enter, the cashier pleaded, "Please, sir, explain to your daughter why she cannot purchase this bird."

Esther stood with her hands cupped before her, a small yellow finch with its head bent low huddled forlornly within. The little bird, obviously sick, rocked back and forth on unsteady legs in the web of Esther's fingers, its eyes closed to slits and bright head nodding as if to a mournful dirge. "C'mon, Ess," said Marshall, "please don't do this. Can't you pick another?"

Stern faced, angry, Esther stamped her sneakered foot and drew the bird closer to her chest. Turning his gaze to the toe-tapping saleslady, Marshall explained how it had long been their custom to rescue injured creatures, no matter their condition, and nurse them back to health. From the impatient look on the woman's face, he could see she wasn't impressed, that for her it was a question of liability, of store policy, and that Esther's efforts at upholding tradition didn't stand a chance. But everyone deserves a chance, Marshall thought, even this sorry little bird. And so, leaning forward with his hands on the counter, he tried to win over the reluctant woman by appealing to her sense of compassion. In the middle of his diatribe, his oral history of the many animals Esther and her mom had tried—and failed—to rescue, he realized that his posture and bloody right hand was frightening the poor young woman, who shrank back warily from the looming figure of this raggedy, pitch-smelling logger. A man, he thought, an angry man; where had he hidden his squirt gun?

Turning away, he looked at Esther and lowered his face to hers. "Put it back, Essie. It's just gonna die. There's some things you just can't save."

Without saying a word Esther turned on her heel and strode down the aisle to the birds' cage. Kneeling beside it, she opened its door and placed the sad finch on the newspaper floor exactly where she had found it. Rising abruptly, she brushed past Marshall without ever meeting his eyes. Reprising his custom of sighing out loud, Marshall nodded to the hapless salesgirl while struggling to show her a smile, greeted only by silence and stone-faced rebuff for his efforts at phony placation. The merry little tinkle of the opening door belied his more honest emotions, as he followed Esther back into the night and whatever remained of their evening.

Back in the truck, Esther leaned on her door with her arms crossed high on her chest. Staring out the window—and away from Marshall—her posture spoke louder than words.

"Listen, Ess," Marshall began, but Esther bolted upright in her seat and leaned in close to his face. "Why did you let her do that!" she growled. "That poor little bird will die all alone! No one will be there to help it!"

Marshall's breath felt sucked from his lungs, the words he'd been forming left stranded midair like a tablecloth yanked from beneath them. Opening his mouth to defend himself, he quickly shut it again and sat there gazing out the grimy windshield wondering what the fuck had just happened. Even the monkey was staring him down from the small portal rubbed on the glass, the knowing eyes of the animal gods focused in harsh condemnation. Turning the key, engaging a gear, Marsh pulled out of the parking lot and back onto Friday night State Street, where a stream of bright headlights quickly engulfed them, sweeping them up in its current.

A couple of minutes and half a mile later, Esther ventured, "Say something, Marshall. Don't just sit there. You're getting all spooky again."

"And ugly," he added, for clarity's sake. "Remember? The scabs and dirty fingernails? Ugly and weird, you said."

"And silly," she amended, silly coming closest to describing her thoughts about Marshall, the confusing, uncomfortable feeling she got from him sometimes. Just when she thought she knew what he was thinking he'd say something, do something that didn't make sense, didn't fit with her concept of who he was and what she could expect from him.

"That's me," he agreed. "I've been thinking weird, silly things about you all day."

"Me?" she said. "How come?"

"The thing with the monkey, and then the dead bird—"

"The bird was not dead!"

"Ever since reading that fortune cookie, the one about your dad—"

"My father? What are you talking about, Marshall? You really are silly. You truly are weird sometimes."

Crushed, dispirited, the behavioral theories he'd been constructing all day reduced to smoking ash, Marshall sought atonement. "I'm sorry, Ess," he said. "I guess I thought you were bummed about something. I thought you were maybe depressed."

It was Esther's turn to be silent, to stare out the window at the lights on the water, the way they bounced on the waves. She had to admit she'd been mad at the lady at the pet store, acting all huffy and superior like that, like grownups often do. But she hadn't been acting weird about stuff, no more than most people did.

"I'm depressed?" she said. "I'm the one who's sad? You're the one moping around all day with Beth Ann's letter in your pocket. Here," she said, attempting to snatch it out, "let me read it for you!"

"Hey," he shouted, slapping at her hand. "Mind your fucking boundaries!"

Marshall often swore around Esther—"I'm a fucking logger!" he'd once explained. "And also from New York!" But the way he said it now surprised her; it even scared her somehow.

Pulling into a turnout above Boulevard Park, Marshall killed the engine. It ticked and groaned as the highlights dimmed until he killed them too, and in the absence of light the bay appeared, a great black void stretching west. Drawing a breath, he eventually said, "I don't need to read it 'cause I know what it says. How she'll never forget me. How she hopes we'll be friends. The same old shit people say."

"But what if it doesn't!" Esther countered. "What if it says she'll love you forever and will never leave Glacier again!"

Marshall sighed and shrugged his shoulders, thinking how kids could be so smart but also dumb as a stump. Not really dumb but unworldly, naïve, or just more charitable than adults. He felt at that moment like a small, yellow bird that Esther was trying to save, feeding his ego for one more day before waking up stiff in the sawdust.

"You know Beth Ann," he said, "the way she writes, a thousand words that say nothing at all, or everything at once. I might not ever know what she means until I see her again. If I see her again."

"Then call her! Call her right now! There's a phone booth right over there!" said Esther, pointing across the dimly lit parking area.

"C'mon, Ess…"

"You c'mon, Marshall! Stop being a mope. Man up and act like a logger!"

He might have laughed had he not felt so ashamed, reprimanded by a kid who still wore braces, who showed far more courage than he.

"Fine," said Esther, reaching for the door latch, "then I'll call her!"

"Wait!" he shouted. "I'll call, okay? But you stay here or I'll never be able to talk."

Patting her head to make her stay, as if she was some kind of dog, Marshall unfolded himself from the cab and headed toward the glow of the phone booth.

Not forty feet away, lit up like a space capsule, the accordion door of the booth stood open like a snapping, salivating jaw. Rifling through his pants for change, disappointed he wasn't wearing the pair with holes in all the pockets, he entered the narrow enclosure, stacked a tower of quarters atop the telephone book, and paused with his finger on the keypad. Hazarding a backward glance at the truck, he saw Esther slide into the driver's seat, the better to monitor his actions. "Jesus weeps," he mumbled aloud, his own eyes suddenly damp. Slowly, solemnly, he began the process of inserting coins in the slot, each ding like the tolling of a gothic bell until finally the dial tone buzzed. Punching Beth's number, his stomach churned and his heart beat hard in his chest, filled with anxiety for what he might hear and what he might say in return. He found himself wishing she'd be in the shower and wouldn't hear the telephone ring, granting a de facto form of reprieve, if only for an hour or another whole day, one more minute of hope. But what would it mean if she didn't answer, if her car in the driveway with its doors opened wide wasn't a sign of Beth's return but only of her packing more stuff?

Whatever the reason, the phone kept ringing and Marshall let it drone on, playing for time or a clue what to say when he had to return to the truck. On the back of the phonebook where his quarters were stacked, a phone number scribbled in loopy red ink caught his divided attention, and feigning to scratch at the ruff of his beard, he stealthily fingered the disconnect switch and slid another coin in the slot. Dialing the number, glancing at the truck, the phone rang twice and a youthful voice answered. "Shakey's Pizza," a bored kid recited. "How may I help you this evening?"

Esther watched Marshall end the call, pause, and dial again. What was he up to now, she thought? Who was he trying to fool? She felt so sorry for Marshall sometimes, for the obvious, transparent things he did in disguising the truth of his feelings. It was that silly part of him, the part that didn't fit with the beard and the swear words, the smoke he blew out through his nose. She still couldn't believe he'd let her drive the truck, right there in the middle of Bellingham! People made Marshall do what they wanted. Girls did, really. Yeah, girls. Her mom had always done it, and Beth Ann did it all the time. Esther had done it too, was doing it right now! Girls bossed Marshall around, not men, and he let them. He couldn't refuse.

Esther felt bad that he was out there now, talking to Beth on the phone, maybe hearing that she didn't love him anymore, maybe feeling that he couldn't be loved. She knew how that felt, and she wished with all her heart that she had let him buy her some little creature, a healthy bird, a salamander, a fish in a baggie full of water. And she hadn't really tricked him into letting her drive; she couldn't help crying, her tears had been real. It was just that stupid old fortune cookie . . . and her even stupider father.

Closing her eyes, squeezing them tight, the tiniest tear escaped her long lashes and trickled its way down one cheek.

"Yeah, sure," Marshall agreed, "Canadian bacon, and pineapple too, though I hate all that crap on a pizza. Yeah, right by the steps that go down to the park. A white Datsun pickup truck."

Turning his back toward where Essie was watching, he fingered the switch till the line went dead, but kept the phone pressed to his cheek. "Hey, it's me," he spoke into the mouthpiece, "just figured I better check in. I saw your car pulled up to your house but didn't have time to stop by. I got your letter right here in my pocket . . . I just haven't opened it yet. Can't really say I'm surprised you're leaving, 'cause I always figured you would. Don't guess we could ever be more to each other than what we are right now. Not that what we had wasn't much, 'cause it sure was plenty for me. You probably need more than a one-horse town and a cowboy who can't ride horses, though I'd much rather think it was Glacier that bored you and not ol' predictable me. But there it is, 'cause you're leaving us both, and not looking back, I suppose. Looking back's always been a problem for me, the fact that I do it too often. Guess I can take that much from our time, all the hours we spent together. 'Be here now,' the gurus say, but they don't hold a candle to you. I'll be okay once it all sinks in, in a month or a decade from now.

"So, I gotta go, 'cause the pizza is coming. Essie says hi, by the way. What's that? Oh yeah, I remember that time. The sky was so blue, and the flowers . . ."

Slipping the receiver back on its hook, he could feel the definitive click, ending the call as if closing a book—though keeping his place with one finger. Released from the booth and its prism of light—a freight train rumbled somewhere in the dark, buoy lights bounced on the waves. Drawing a draught of the cool night air, he figured he just might quit smoking.

"What did she say?" asked Esther, climbing back into the passenger seat.

"Oh, Ess, what didn't she say," Marshall groaned, slumping behind the wheel.

"Who wants to know what she didn't say! Are you gonna tell me or not?"

"Sure I will, but not right now. How 'bout you roll me a smoke," he deflected, his oath to forego the nasty habit betrayed in just under a minute.

Sucking in air in prelude to whining, Esther thought better of it and held her breath, resolving to be kinder to Marshall.

"Where is it?" she asked.

"Where's what?"

"The tobacco!" she growled, coming close to blowing her cool already.

"It's there on the dash in front of you."

"Oh," she said, feeling sheepish, admonished, and fell quickly to the task of rolling.

Fumbling with the paper, pinching at tobacco, her thoughts were as distant and far away as the lights way out on the islands. She'd ruined their precious night out together, rebuffing Marshall's every attempt to be nice to her, ignoring him at the pet store, giving all her attention to the monkey and then that lonely bird. What little kid doesn't like pet stores? No wonder no one wanted to be her father.

Marsh felt like dog shit. He'd just perpetuated a massive fraud and felt nothing but contempt for himself. No wonder he bored Beth Ann. How could anyone continue to love him once they found out what a cowardly, fearful person he truly was. Beth wanted challenge, excitement, engagement, to charge through life with a dauntless resolve and the courage of a million puppies! Yes, even puppies were better people than Marshall.

He was slumming again, wallowing in self-pity. But it wasn't just indulgence this time; it was reality, facing up to those truths about himself that he'd always sought to hide behind a veneer of masculinity, of cultural norms wherein men weren't obliged to reveal their true feelings but hold them inside like a secret. But eventually those secrets morphed into lies, withheld for so long that the not-telling of them became deceitful, became dishonest, became privileged. Marsh was the man that Beth Ann so despised; was she just now beginning to see it?

"Here," Esther mumbled, holding the roll-your-own up to the light. It was poorly constructed, hastily assembled, resembling a banana, or an ear of corn in profile.

"Thanks," said Marshall, snatching it from her, striking a match in the cup of his hands.

In the brief incandescence of sulfurous light, Esther's pale face was illumined, much like that of the sad little monkey holding its hand to the glass. "Marshall," she said when the darkness returned, a hesitant tone in her voice, "do you think of me as your daughter?"

All thoughts of honesty, of ending the lies, fell away like fresh snow from a tree branch, leaving only the droopiest, slenderest twig of the man he pretended to be. What did he know about honesty and truth, about the price of each or the value of anything? He did know about need, felt that he'd cornered the market on it. And he knew what Esther wanted to hear, but how could he say it after all the years and countless last chances gone by? What could a childless, middle-aged man know about loving a daughter?

And just as he was about to speak, the match still smoking in his fingers, a little red pickup with an oven in its bed pulled up beside his window. "You order a pizza?" a voice called over a loudspeaker.

Marsh flinched at the sound, a look of pain like a blow from an axe drawing his eyes into slits. Glancing at Esther, her face was a mask as she slowly absorbed what he'd done, a vague recognition transforming her features like stones skipped over a pond.

"Huh," she said, "how did someone know I was dying for pizza?"

So they sat in the truck and ate the pizza with barely a word spoken, Marsh plucking chunks of pineapple from his slices, piling them all on Esther's. She didn't eat much, leaving the scalloped crescents of crust to litter the box like old bones. He smoked the cigarette Essie had rolled, and she rolled him another for the long drive home in case she fell asleep. Which she did, rather promptly, leaving Marshall alone with his thoughts, puffing on that butt as the Datsun took the long curve by the Highway 9 cutoff, leaving the flats and the farmlands behind as they entered the domain of the mountains.

Laid out across the console with her head on Marshall's hip, Esther appeared to be dreaming, her golden hair glowing in the dashboard lights, her thin lips moving, eyelashes fluttering, her breath coming steady and slow. Many was the night Beth Ann had lain that way, in the same sleepy depths of innocence and trust, with the same greenish glow on her cheeks. Tentatively reaching to stroke Esther's hair, Marshall recalled his own waking dreams that had colored his thoughts in those moments, floating up now like his own private butterflies to flit through the smoke of the cab.

He pictured Beth naked as they sat at a cliff's edge, another ridge rising precipitously before them. "Valleys are like mountains inside out," she'd observed, "and we're perched upside down on their underneath bottoms with clouds sailing under our toes."

Another time, on another ridgetop, Marshall and Beth had watched the sun setting, a purplish cloud at the curve of the Earth, and Beth Ann imagined it as a huge black eye, a bruise-colored shiner just moments since being punched out. She'd described winter branches as India ink spilled from the nib of a pen, wildflowers as terribly slow-moving kaleidoscopes, waterfalls as cracks in a broken window, their edges lit up by the sun.

One time, driving down the highway, she'd explained that when her trusty Volkswagen finally died it would sound like silverware— knives, forks, and spoons—falling out of the bottom of the car. In the very next instant, a mere breath removed, she'd asked Marsh if he'd ever tried chewing gum on both sides of his mouth at the same time.

She'd claimed she could never clean her house without dressing up in some costume, playing her music cranked to the max to drown out the sound of the vacuum. Marsh knew this to be true, as he'd sat many times at her kitchen counter drinking coffee, reading Beth's fashion magazines, listening to the Indigo girls as she scurried around wearing nothing but high heels and a red T-shirt that had Ladies Sewing Circle and Terrorist Society printed on the front. Another time she'd worn a Mariner's ball cap, an Army surplus rain poncho, and Marshall's knee-high rubber boots. "Once," she recalled, "my house was so filthy I had to wear my black satin jazz pants, rhinestone sunglasses, and do my hair in a French braid."

What would Marsh do without all that? He couldn't recall how he'd survived before it, couldn't imagine a world where the sun rose and set without reminding anyone of a big black eye, where people walked around oblivious to the upside-down, inside-out possibilities of the earth beneath their feet. Shivering at the thought, he lowered his hand with its mutilated thumb and stroked Esther's baby soft hair. She sighed in her sleep and snuggled in closer, obstructing the gearshift knob. But Marsh didn't care, and leaving the tranny to struggle in fourth, he lugged it up the grade toward Maple Falls, growing more apprehensive as the miles clicked by and Glacier, and his fate, drew nearer.

What would he do if when he arrived Beth's car was not parked in her driveway, if the porch lights were out and the curtains drawn, just the crazy old maypole, now weathered gray, leaning sideways on the spare patch of lawn?

Marshall had cut that pole himself, had dug the hole and hoisted it aloft with long streamers trailing like a tepee. It had been a hard time for both of them. They were "needing some space," exploring their options, the first real manifestation of their divergent dreams. Beth had done extensive research on Mayday celebrations, even getting the staff at the local library involved, and her little house was filled with accordion music, flower baskets, and bottles of German wine. She'd invited the whole town, her position as bartender at

Graham's the literal root of the Glacier grapevine, and the whole town was eager to attend. But first she had needed a Maypole, and she knew just the right guy to find one. It was an awkward conversation when Marsh volunteered, and he was glad to be off on his mission, away from the gaiety of the gathering crowd and the cheerful bunting that Beth had draped all around.

He had driven up to the log landing where he'd been working earlier in the day, now deserted and peaceful in early evening. Small birds flitted from branch to shattered branch in the crow's nest of detritus surrounding the muddy flat, squirrels chittered angrily at the edge of the timber, the monstrous shovel and towering yarder eerily silent in repose. As the westering sun shone green through the treetops, he was struck by the contrast the place offered. Here, and in places like it, he was spending his life, a life filled solely with men, far from the crystal and long-stemmed roses with which Beth surrounded herself. His was a world of scraggly beards and easy, spittle-toothed smiles, haggard faces in battered tin hats telling terrible jokes in the crummy. Often brutal, always extreme, logging was a job where men toiled daily in the absolute worst of conditions, where the world was pitched at near vertical angles, so close to the earth that mud caked in your beard and pitch clung in beads to your hair. There was something primal about it, ancient, and tribal. You could taste it in your sweat, see it in a smile, hear it in a torrent of swear words, feel it in the sudden give of the lines as males of the species bent to their task and pulled until it hurt. What was so wrong with that, he wondered. What was so macho about wanting to feel one's primitive, animal self? Didn't anyone out there want to believe that men's lives could be beautiful too?

Marshall had returned with the maypole, erected it with colorful streamers flowing, and stood watching from the periphery as Beth led the contingent of laughing kids and inebriated adults around the pole, in and out of each other's paths in jubilant imprecision. It ended with Beth Ann tied to the pole, wound in a lacing of crepe paper ribbons—sky-blue, yellow, and pink.

She looked so beautiful in her white cotton blouse and billowing turquoise skirt, so joyous and youthful and willfully bound as the whole town danced around her. Never had Marshall felt so distant, so ugly and alone, the scars and scabs on his forearms and wrists inscribed like prison tattoos. He waited for a chance to catch Beth alone, but the moment never arrived, and he slipped away quietly in his crappy old pickup without ever saying goodbye.

And now, as that same crappy Datsun rolled through Glacier, Marshall's worst fears were realized, as no green-and-white Volkswagen sat in Beth's driveway and no lights burned in her window, just the maypole, leaning in silent rebuke with its crepe paper streamers gone limp. Chugging past the library/post office, past Graham's Restaurant/Store, he coasted down the street to the last and only house on the block where a single, yellow bug light cast its pale oval on the porch. Killing the engine he sat there a moment, Esther still asleep on his lap. He studied her beautiful, innocent face, her ivory complexion and rounded cheeks. Soon her cheekbones would grow pronounced, and her child's nose more refined, and before she knew it she'd be a young woman, capable of breaking a young man's heart, susceptible to her own being broken. He wished he could save her from such a fate but knew that it was futile, and he wondered if other creatures—the wolves and eagles that mated for life—struggled with their emotions, their sense of loss, their reason for living beyond just the instinct for survival.

"Ess," he whispered, squeezing her shoulder. "We're home. Time to wake up."

Esther was not one to dally in dreams, and she sat up immediately, her face puffy, eyes swimming but expressionless. The look she gave Marshall was devoid of intent, absent of thought, innocently focused on the weary eyes of a not-so-innocent man whose own thoughts were far from empty, filled in fact with a waking dream he desperately sought to escape.

"G'night," said Esther, fumbling with the door latch.

"Thanks for the . . ." she began, about to say movie, or dinner, realizing they'd not really done either.

"Sure," said Marshall before she could speak, equally incapable of defining what they'd accomplished that evening.

Climbing from the truck, pausing on the porch, Esther glanced back from the doorway; she gave him a wave, he returned it with a smile, and the door clicked shut behind her.

When the porch light blinked off, a loneliness descended so profound, so enveloping, that Marsh felt he'd somehow been wired to the light switch, an emotional, Tesla-like energy field wherein he was the single electrode. The warmly lit windows of the few houses around him glowed as if in mockery, the people within them secure in the knowledge that their lives would continue unchanged, that the next day brought nothing but sunrise and sameness as they went about their daily routines.

Turning the ignition key, popping the clutch, the Datsun jerked and stalled, jerked and stalled as he bellowed profanities within the muffled confines of the cab, eventually succeeding in attaining second gear. Circumnavigating the block, pulling the grade to the intersection of the highway, he almost laughed at the tableau presented, the proverbial fork in the road. Not really a fork, but T-bone shaped—more perpendicular in nature—he nevertheless recognized the choice presented: turn east up the mountain toward his cold little cabin to sulk in his overstuffed chair, staring at the photo from Valentine's Day by the light of a kerosene lamp; or hang a quick right toward Beth Ann's house where he knew the back door would be open, check to see if she'd actually left and was not just gone for the weekend. But what if the place was empty and silent, just a hair tie or sock on the floor, a few cardboard boxes, a half cup of coffee gone cold on the bare kitchen counter?

Popping the clutch up onto the highway, the truck hitched violently and stalled again, rolling to a lurching, inelegant stop on the graveled shoulder of the road. His facility with stick shifts permanently impaired, Marsh burst from the cab with its door sprung wide and strode in a circle beneath the only streetlamp in town, his methodical orbit slowly decreasing until finally, his energy depleted, he plopped down on the steps of the library/ post office where the damp boards soaked through the seat of his pants. In dire need of a cigarette, he whipped out his nearly depleted pouch of tobacco and rolled the lumpiest, crookedest, bloodiest cigarette a man might be tempted to smoke. Stuffing the cleaner end in his mouth, he futilely searched for a match, standing again to turn out his pockets as sawdust fluttered to the ground, along with the paycheck he'd forgotten to cash, but still no goddam matches. "Gimme fuckin' strength," he mumbled, one hand reaching to explore his shirt pocket where he touched the crisp edge of Beth's letter.

"No fuckin' way," he swore out loud. "Might as well burn it right now."

Possessed of an even greater need for fire, he fingered through the pocket, barely noticing the flutter of a pink slip of paper as it tried to escape on the breeze. Reflexively snatching it out of the air—mindful of it hitting the ground—he held it to the light of the lonely streetlamp and struggled to read its inscription. Still damp with saliva from the driving lesson when he'd almost swallowed it whole, he read its message for real this time, holding his breath as he did so: *A Pond has no bottom for those who would swim*, the cryptic poet informed him. "Who writes this shit," he wondered aloud, "Lao Tzu, or Sylvia Plath?" And throwing all caution to the listless wind, if not Beth's letter itself, he plopped back down on the frozen stairs and tore the envelope open. It began without preamble, no Dear Marshall, Dear Sir, or even To Whom It May Concern:

> Remember that day in the grocery store
> when we were trying to pick out a cantaloupe?
> A nice old woman showed us how to shake
> them to see if they were ripe, to hear if they
> were hollow inside, and we shook them all like
> castanets, rhumba-ing around in the produce

aisle. Outside in the sunshine, sitting on the grass, we cut one in half and filled it with vanilla ice cream, sharing a crusty, plastic spoon you found on the floor of your truck. It was messy and sticky eating ice cream in the heat, and you crawled on your knees to kiss drips from my chin, ignoring the stares from passing shoppers who looked like they wanted cantaloupe too. We talked about gardening, movies, and hiking, and you looked so happy—*we* were so happy that day. I told you how much I wanted to act, to learn to dance, and maybe even fly airplanes. You smiled through it all as we crumpled up napkins, scattered like flowers on the grass. But I could tell by the look in your eyes how much it hurt you to listen, to hear all the things that would take me away from you and the mountains you loved. I pretended not to see it, and you pretended not to care, though both of us knew what would happen in the end, that an end would eventually arrive.

The very first night we spent together we didn't even take off our clothes, just snuggled and kissed and fell asleep to the sound of the creek through a window. You were gone in the morning, and I went to work wondering if you'd come back. You did, of course, with a bouquet of flowers you'd picked on the trail to Twin Lakes—purple lupine, snow white daisies, ruby red Indian paintbrush. You were sunburned and brown and your skin felt hot when we finally got naked that night, the heat of our bodies in the oven of blankets baking our sweat like a glaze. Brown skin, bright flowers, clear blue sky, the breath-taking thrill of cold water . . . that's what you gave me, what I'll never forget, now that our cantaloupe's gone.

You can blame me for everything, and I wish you would because sometimes I know I deserve it. Does that sound flaky? Does it sound just like me, the girl who can't make up her mind? You think I'm just young, and I let you believe it, but really our age makes no difference. Your love was so sweet, like the love of a child, and we acted like two little kids. But most of the time I don't know what I want, and that's how I'm different from you. You already have what you're looking for, but it's like you're afraid to believe it. You think you want me, and work so hard to prove it, and I've never felt so desired. I wanted it too. I *loved* you too, and here comes the part where I say it—I will *always* love you, I truly will, and although I know how it hurts you to hear it, I also know you believe me.

I'm not leaving you, Marshall, and neither did Karen, or any of the people you've loved. *You* aren't the reason that people move on, pass on to whatever's ahead. It's life, not loss, so stop blaming yourself like I'm blaming myself right now. I picture your face as you're reading this letter, and you're picturing me as I write it. So look at me, Marshall, look in my eyes when I tell you how much I felt loved, how you taught me to love, and to give love back as hard and as fast as you gave it. So goodbye my lover, my logger, my man, my genuine male among men.
Alllllllll my love, Beth Ann

Marsh didn't bother to read it again. It was true that he'd already known what it would say, but it just sounded better when Beth Ann said it. How did she do that, he had to wonder. Was she really that much smarter than him, or just more willing to say stuff out loud? Stuffing the letter back in the envelope, he returned it to the pocket of his shirt where, behold and lo, he discovered a book of matches. Lighting the cigarette, he sucked in a drag with the vengeance of draining a snake bite, then puffed out a trembling oval of smoke to lasso a cluster of stars. The night had grown chilly while his mind was away, and he couldn't tell his breath from the smoke, the seat of his pants now stuck to the wood by a tenuous rime of ice. But Marsh was immune to that kind of stuff and could easily have fallen asleep, which he almost did, folding both arms across his knees and laying his head in their cradle.

Within that darkness his mind spun around in mandala-like 3D collage, like a Busby Berkeley overhead shot from a corny Hollywood musical. Kaleidoscopic images of cantaloupes and jellybeans ran superimposed through each frame, a spiraling vortex of maypole ribbons and Vaseline jars full of nickels, black eye sunsets, broken toes, bubble bath rainbows in the mist, memories rising unsummoned to the surface of a place just below conscious thought.

And these were Marshall's conscious thoughts: Love was intangible, inscrutable, inescapable as it swept through one's life like a current. And just like high voltage, few people touched it without making sure they were grounded, without clinging to what-ifs, maybes, or buts before plugging their life into another. Fewer still thought of love as their savior; Jesus had, and look what happened to him. But even Christ couldn't love the whole world without first loving one other person, that face in the crowd as he stumbled up Calvary with the weight of the world on his shoulders, shifting the cross from side to side for one last look in her eyes. Or *his* eyes even. What did Marsh care! Who was a logger to judge?

That was the way of the world, he knew, and the path to a broken heart, aortas and ventricles scattered on the black top like silverware spilled from a car. He hoped that wouldn't happen to Beth in her quest for more people to love, speeding down the highway in her trusty green Bug with a diving board song in her heart, rhinestone sunglasses aimed at the sun as she tapped out a rhythm on the gas pedal. And maybe once she had tilted at windmills and jousted with ass-pinching dragons, she'd remember that sock she'd left on the floor and pilot her plane back to Glacier, where she might drop a letter in Marshall's box suggesting they go on a hike, up to Keep Kool to float in a lake with their toes sticking out of the water.

Maintaining that image of sun on his face and hard nipples piercing the surface, Marsh felt warm fingers slip into his hand,

and at first he refused to look up. Don't move, don't ruin it, he cautioned himself, prolong it as long as you can. Hope was a wonderful, terrible thing, depending on how it was offered, as a promise of the future or a crutch for the present, both too painful to ponder. Wondering which option was happening here, he was tempted to dial for a pizza.

Squaring his shoulders, summoning strength, Marshall drew a phlegmy breath and slowly raised his head. Esther stood just inches away with her blonde head cocked to one side, a look both of interest and revulsion on her face, as though observing a threatening bug. She wore an old winter coat he vaguely remembered, puffy and red with a fake fur collar, several seasons and sizes too small for the gangly young woman she'd become. Parting Marshall's calloused fingers, she extracted the butt that had burned to his knuckles and flicked it expertly to land in the grass where smoke spiraled up in the lamp light. Her eyes, so blue, could have been the eyes of any woman, of any age or epoch, and they stared into his with the kind of compassion usually reserved for elders, or at least those well into their teens. And he pictured her several years from now as she struggled her way through high school, then college, then quasi-adulthood, searching for something like wisdom, or love, prowling the produce aisles.

"Don't be afraid of boys," he said.

Esther indulged him with a patient smirk then took his cold hand in hers. "You're just being silly," she let him know, and raising his trembling hand to her lips she kissed the sore tip of his thumb.

In the breadth of that moment with its damp hint of pain, Marshall Thumblood, at age thirty-three, finally became a man. Jesus smiled down from his perch on the cross, a monkey's eye winked in a window, and the dauntless courage of a million puppies swelled his meager chest. "Gross," he deadpanned, repressing a smile, and knew with a certainty gleaned from a lifetime spent vastly outnumbered by girls, that in her own way, and for however briefly, Esther truly did love Carl Ballentine.